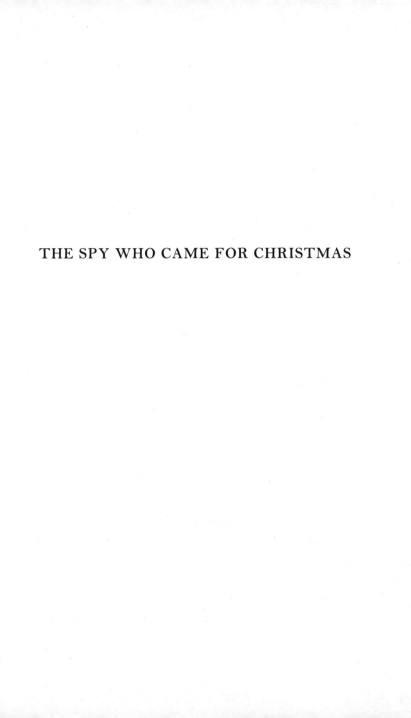

THE SPY WHO CAME FOR CHRISTMAS

Also by David Morrell

NOVELS

First Blood (1972)

Testament (1975)

Last Reveille (1977)

The Totem (1979)

Blood Oath (1982)

The Brotherhood of the Rose (1984)

The Fraternity of the Stone (1985)

Rambo (First Blood Part II) (1985)

The League of Night and Fog (1987)

Rambo III (1988)

The Fifth Profession (1990)

The Covenant of the Flame (1991)

Assumed Identity (1993)

Desperate Measures (1994)

The Totem (Complete and Unaltered) (1994)

Extreme Denial (1996)

Double Image (1998)

Burnt Sienna (2000)

Long Lost (2002)

The Protector (2003)

Creepers (2005)

Scavenger (2007)

SHORT FICTION

The Hundred-Year Christmas (1983)

Black Evening (1999)

Nightscape (2004)

ILLUSTRATED FICTION

Captain America: The Chosen (2007)

NONFICTION

John Barth: An Introduction (1976)

Fireflies: A Father's Tale of Love and Loss (1988)

American Fiction, American Myth (Essays by Philip Young) edited by David Morrell and Sandra Spanier (2000)

The Successful Novelist: A Lifetime of Lessons about Writing and Publishing (2008), revised and expanded version of *Lessons from a Lifetime of Writing: A Novelist Looks at His Craft (2002)*

The
SPY
Who Came for
Christmas

DAVID MORRELL

Vanguard Press
A Member of the Perseus Books Group

Published by Vanguard Press
A Member of the Perseus Books Group

Vanguard Press books are available at special discounts for bulk purchases in the U.S. by corporations, institutions, and other organizations. For more information, please contact the Special Markets Department at Perseus Books Group, 2300 Chestnut Street, Suite 200, Philadelphia, PA 19103, or call (800) 810-4145, ext. 5000, or e-mail special.markets@perseusbooks.com.

Designed by Timm Bryson
Set in 11.5 point Bell

Library of Congress Cataloging-in-Publication Data
Morrell, David.
  The spy who came for Christmas / by David Morrell.
    p. cm.
  ISBN 978-1-59315-487-5
  I. Title.
  PR9199.3.M65S79 2008
  813'.54—dc22

                    2007052579

10 9 8 7 6 5 4 3 2 1

A flower bloomed
In the middle of a cold winter's night,
A rose that Mary gave us,
A small child,
Who dispels the darkness,
Relieves our sorrows,
And saves us from sin and death.

> —paraphrase of a fifteenth-century
> German hymn, "The Christmas Rose"

In the Middle Ages, councils debating confidential matters hung a rose from the ceiling and swore not to reveal what they discussed *sub rosa*, under the rose. This association of a rose with secrecy dates back to a Greek myth in which the god of love gave a rose to the god of silence, bribing him to stay quiet about the sins of the other gods. To this day, the rose remains an emblem of the spy profession.

> —from the *Cambridge Encyclopedia of Espionage*

Part One

The City of Holy Faith

CAROLERS SANG, *"It came upon a midnight clear."*

But it wasn't yet midnight, and it wasn't clear. Snow whispered down, a cold powder that reflected colorful lights hanging on adobe buildings beyond an intersection ahead. Even the traffic lights appeared festive.

"What a perfect Christmas Eve," a woman marveled, proceeding with the crowd on Alameda Street. The Spanish word *alameda* referred to the poplars that had rimmed the street years earlier when it had been only a lane. Although cottonwoods had long since replaced those poplars, the street remained narrow, the sidewalk barely accommodating the crush of people coming from mass at St. Francis Cathedral or from the ice sculptures in Santa Fe's four-hundred-year-old wooded square, known as the Plaza.

"You think the lights in the Plaza are something?" the woman's companion told her. "Wait'll you see Canyon Road. A mile of decorations. You'll be glad you came to visit for the holidays. People travel from all over the world to see Santa Fe at Christmas. You know what it means, don't you? 'Santa Fe'?"

"At the hotel, I heard somebody call it the City Different."

"That's just its nickname. Santa Fe was settled by the Spanish. The name means 'Holy Faith.' It's perfect for this time of year."

"Peace on Earth, goodwill to men . . . "

Moving with the crowd, the man in the black ski jacket didn't care about peace or goodwill. He was forty-five, but the effects of his hard life had made him look older. He had big shoulders and creased features, and he saw with the tunnel vision of a hunter so that objects on each side of him registered only as blurs. For him, sounds diminished as well. The carolers, the cathedral bells, the exclamations of delight at the holiday displays—all of these lessened as he focused solely on his quarry. There were only fifteen people between them.

The target wore a navy parka, but despite the falling snow, he had the hood shoved back, allowing a cold layer of white to accumulate on his head. The pursuer understood. A man on the run couldn't allow the sides of a hood to obstruct his view of what lay on each side. Desperate to find an escape route, the fugitive saw differently than a hunter, not with tunnel vision but with an intense awareness of everything around him.

The killer kept his hands in the pockets of his ski jacket. Inside the pockets were slits that made it easy for him to reach the two pistols he had holstered on his belt under his jacket. Each weapon had a sound suppressor. One was a 10-millimeter Glock, chosen because of its power and because the rifling in Glock barrels blurred the striations on bullets fired from them. As a consequence, crime-scene investigators found it almost impossible to link those bullets to any particular gun.

But if everything went as planned, the force of the Glock wouldn't be necessary. Instead, the second pistol—a .22 Beretta—would be chosen for its subtlety. Even without a suppressor, the small-caliber gun made little noise. But *with* a suppressor, and with subsonic ammunition designed for Santa Fe's 7,000 feet of altitude, the .22 was about as quiet as a pistol could be. Equally important, its lesser power meant that the bullet it fired wasn't likely to jeopardize the mission by going through the target and hitting the precious object hidden under his parka.

"*. . . to hear the angels sing.*"

At the intersection, the traffic light changed to red. As the snow kept falling, the crowd stopped and formed a dense barrier that prevented the hunter from moving closer to his target.

Suddenly, a man's voice blurted from an earbud concealed beneath the black watchman's cap that the hunter wore over his ears.

"Melchior! Status!" the angry voice demanded.

The hunter's name was Andrei. His employer, a former KGB interrogator, had given him the pseudonym "Melchior" to sanitize the team's radio communications in case an enemy accessed their frequency. The seemingly nonsensical choice had puzzled Andrei until he'd learned that, according to tradition, Melchior was one of the wise men who'd followed the Christmas star to Bethlehem and discovered the baby Jesus.

A microphone was concealed under the ski-lift tickets attached to the zipper on Andrei's coat: tickets that were commonplace in this mountain resort. To avoid attracting attention when he replied, he pulled his cell phone from a pants pocket and pretended to talk into it. His breath was white with frost. Although his origins were Russian, his American accent was convincing.

He pressed the microphone to transmit his message.

"Hey, Uncle Harry. I just walked up Alameda Street. I'm on the corner of Paseo de Peralta." The Spanish name meant "walkway of Peralta" and referred to Santa Fe's founder, a governor of New Mexico in the early 1600s. "Canyon Road's across the street. I'll pick up the package and be at your place in twenty minutes."

"Do you know where the package *is*?" The gruff voice made no attempt to conceal its Russian accent, or its impatience.

"Right in front of me," Andrei pretended to say into his cell phone. "The Christmas decorations are amazing."

"Our clients will be here any second. Get it back!"

"As soon as my friends catch up to me."

"Balthazar! Caspar! Status!" the voice demanded.

The unusual pseudonyms were the names that tradition had given to the remaining wise men in the Christmas story.

"Almost there!" another accented voice said through Andrei's earbud, breathing quickly. "When you grab the package, we'll block anybody who gets in the way."

"Good. Tomorrow, we'll watch football," Andrei said into the microphone. "See you in a bit, Uncle Harry."

He wore thin leather shooter's gloves that provided only brief protection from the cold. As the traffic light changed to green, he returned the phone to his pants pocket, then shoved his hands back into his fleece-lined jacket, warming his fingers.

The crowd proceeded across the street, continuing to shield the target, who was about six feet tall, slender but with surprising strength, as Andrei knew firsthand from missions they'd served on together.

And from what had occurred fifteen minutes earlier.

Dark hair of medium length. Rugged yet pleasant features that witnesses otherwise found hard to describe. In his early thirties.

Andrei now realized that these details were the extent of what he knew about the man. The thought intensified his anger. Until tonight, he'd believed that he and his quarry were on the same side—and more, that they were friends.

You're the only person I trusted, Pyotyr. How many other lies did you tell? I vouched for you. I told the Pakhan that he could depend on you. If I don't get back what you stole, he'll have me killed.

The man reached the opposite side of the street and turned to the right, passing star-shaped lights strung along the windows of an art gallery. Andrei shifted a little closer—only thirteen people away now—avoiding sudden movements, doing nothing that would disrupt the flow of the crowd and cause his prey to look back. Although the man's gait remained steady, Andrei knew that his left arm was wounded. It hung at his side. Shadows and trampling footsteps concealed the blood he left on the snow.

You'll soon weaken, Andrei thought, surprised that he hadn't already.

Red and blue lights flashed ahead, making Andrei tense. Despite the holiday surroundings, it was impossible to mistake those lights for Christmas displays. Reflected by the falling snow, they were mounted on the roofs of two police cars that blocked the entrance to Canyon Road. Large red letters on the cars' white doors announced, SANTA FE POLICE.

Andrei's shoulders tightened. *Are they searching for us? Have they found the bodies?*

Two burly policemen in bulky coats stood before the cruisers, stamping their boots in the snow, trying to keep warm. Stiff from the cold, they awkwardly raised their left arms and motioned toward oncoming headlights, warning cars and pickup trucks to keep going and not enter Canyon Road.

Ahead in the crowd, a woman pointed with concern. "Why would the police be here? Something must have happened. Maybe we'd better stay away."

"Nothing's wrong," her companion assured her. "The police form a barricade every year. Christmas Eve, cars can't drive on Canyon Road. Only pedestrians are allowed there tonight."

Andrei watched Pyotyr walk around the cruisers and enter the celebration on Canyon Road, taking care to avoid eye contact with the policemen. They paid him no attention, looking bored.

Yes, they're only managing traffic, Andrei decided. *That'll soon change, but by then, I'll have what I need and be out of here.*

He wondered why Pyotyr hadn't run to the police for help, but after a moment's thought, he understood. *The bastard knows we won't allow anything to stop us from taking back what he stole. With their weapons holstered, those two cops wouldn't have a chance if we rushed them.*

Staring ahead, he noticed how the increasing narrowness of Canyon Road made the crowd even denser. Santa Fe was a small city of about 70,000 people. Before beginning his assignment, Andrei had reconnoitered the compact downtown area and knew that Canyon Road had few side streets. It reminded him of a funnel.

Things will happen swiftly now, he thought. *I'll get you, my friend.*

Whoever you are.

Andrei's vision narrowed even more, focusing almost exclusively on the back of Pyotyr's head, where he intended to put his bullet. Pretending to marvel at the Christmas decorations, he passed the flashing lights of the police cars and entered the kill zone.

THE MAN WHO called himself Pyotyr saw with intense clarity, all of his senses operating at their fullest, taking in everything around him.

Canyon Road was lined with mostly single-story buildings, many of which boasted pueblo-revival architecture, their flat roofs, rounded edges, and earth-colored stucco so distinctive that visitors marveled. The majority of the buildings—some of them dating back to the eighteenth century—had been converted into art galleries, hundreds of them, making this street one of the most popular art scenes in the United States.

Tonight, their outlines were emphasized by countless flickering candles—what the locals called *farolitos*—that were set in sand poured into paper bags and placed next to walkways. Some of the candles had been knocked over accidentally, the paper bags burning, but most remained intact, their shimmer not yet affected by the settling snow.

Bonfires lit each side of the road, their occasional loud crackles causing him to flinch as if from gunshots. The wood they burned had been cut from pine trees known as piñons, and the fragrant smoke reminded him of incense.

Your mind's drifting, he warned himself, trying to ignore the pain in his arm. *Forget the damned smoke. Pay attention. Find a way out of here.*

His real name was Paul Kagan, but over the years, in other places, he had used many other names. Tonight, he'd decided to become himself.

The left pocket of his parka was torn open, the result of someone grabbing for him when he'd escaped. He recalled the shock he'd felt when he'd reached for his cell phone and discovered that it had fallen out. Something had seemed to fall inside him as well. Without a way to contact his controller, he was powerless to summon help.

Kagan wore a flesh-colored earbud, so small that it was almost impossible to notice in the shadows. A miniature microphone was hidden on his parka, but all communication had stopped fifteen minutes earlier. He took for granted that his hunters had switched to a new frequency to prevent him from eavesdropping while they searched for him.

Doing his best to blend with the crowd, he strained to be aware of everything around him: the carolers, the twinkling lights on the galleries and the trees, the art dealers offering steaming cocoa to passersby. He searched for an escape route but knew that if the men chasing him managed to follow him to a quiet area, he wouldn't have a chance.

Nor would the object he held under his parka.

He felt it squirm. Fearful that it might be smothered, he pulled the zipper down far enough to provide air. It might be making sounds, but the carols and conversations around him prevented him from knowing for sure. Those same distractions prevented the crowd from hearing what he hid under his coat.

"We three kings of Orient are . . . "

Yeah, they came from the East all right, Kagan thought. In his weakened condition, the incense-like smell of the bonfires reminded him of the gifts the three Magi had brought to the baby Jesus: frankincense for a priest, gold for a king, and myrrh, an embalming perfume for one who is to die.

But not what's under my parka, Kagan thought. *By God, I'll do anything to make sure* it *doesn't die.*

"PAUL, WE HAVE *a new assignment for you. How's your Russian?"*

"It's good, sir. My parents were afraid to speak it, even in secret. But after the Soviet Union collapsed, all of a sudden it was the only language they spoke around the house. The urge to use it had built up during the years they were in hiding. I needed to learn Russian so I could understand what they said."

"Your file says they defected to the United States in 1976."

"That's right. They were part of the Soviet gymnastics team sent to the summer Olympics in Montreal. They managed to slip away

from their handlers, reached the American consulate, and requested political asylum."

"Interesting that they chose the U.S. instead of Canada."

"I think they worried that Canada's winters would be as cold as those in their former home in Leningrad."

"I was hoping you'd tell me they admired the American way of life."

"They did, sir, especially Florida, where they went to live and never felt cold again."

"Florida? I had an assignment there one Christmas. All that sun and sand, the mood didn't work. They never felt cold? I assume you mean except for the Cold War."

"Yes, sir. The Soviets never stopped searching for defectors, especially ones who'd made international headlines. Despite the new identities the State Department gave them, my parents were always afraid they'd be tracked down."

"Their original names were Irina and Vladimir Kozlov?"

"Correct."

"Changed to Kagan?"

"Yes, sir. Gymnastics was their passion, but they soon realized they could never compete again. The risk of discovery was too great. They didn't even dare go into a gymnasium and practice their moves. They knew they wouldn't be able to resist doing their best, and if people saw how amazing they were, word would have spread. Perhaps to the wrong people. My parents were too terrified to take the chance. Suppressing their talents broke their spirit. That was the price of their freedom."

"They could have won gold medals?"

"Almost certainly. But they defected because of me. Relationships between male and female gymnasts were strictly forbidden, but somehow they managed to find time to sneak away and be by themselves. Perhaps if the opportunity hadn't seemed so rare, they might not have . . . Well, in any case, when my mother realized she was pregnant, she knew that the Soviets would insist she have an abortion, to keep her in competition. She was determined not to let that happen."

"Only teenagers—they grew up fast."

"They were so paranoid about KGB agents grabbing us in the middle of the night that they raised me to be suspicious of everyone, to study everything wherever I went, and to watch for anybody who seemed out of place. As I grew up, I thought it was a normal way to live, always keeping secrets."

"So it was natural for you to become a spy."

"COLE'S BEEN throwing up," the man said into the telephone, taking care not to make his words sound forced. "Some kind of stomach bug. I'm afraid we can't come to the party. . . . Yes, I'm sorry, too. It's an awful way to spend Christmas Eve. . . . I'll tell him. Thanks."

He pressed the dial-tone button, then picked up a hammer from the counter and smashed the phone into pieces—just as he'd done with the phone in his office and the one in the master bedroom.

Chunks of plastic flew across the kitchen.

"There," the man said unsteadily. He dropped the hammer, opened a woman's purse that was lying on the counter, and took out a cell phone, shoving it into his coat pocket. "That takes care of everything." He crossed the kitchen and yanked open the side door, the motion so violent that it sucked snow into the house. While the flakes settled over the woman lying on the floor, he raged outside and slammed the door behind him.

Pressed against a kitchen cupboard, the boy was so stunned that for a moment he couldn't speak. Finally, he found his voice.

"Mom?" Tears burned his eyes. "Are you okay?" He moved toward her. Although the heel on his right shoe was higher than the one on the left, it didn't fully compensate for his short right leg, giving him a slight limp.

He knelt and touched her arm, feeling dampness where the snow that had blown in was already melting on her.

"I'm . . ." His mother took a deep breath and found the strength to raise herself to a sitting position. "I'm . . . going to be all right." Her right hand touched the side of her cheek, causing her to wince. "Get me . . . some ice cubes, would you, sweetheart? Put them in a dishcloth."

Moving quickly despite his limp, the boy grabbed a dish towel from the counter and went to the side-by-side. He tugged the freezer door open, reaching in. The ice cubes chilled his fingers. While his mother groaned, making the effort to stand, he wrapped the ice cubes in the towel and hurried back to her.

"You're always a help," she murmured. "I don't know what I'd do without you." She put the ice pack against her cheek. Blood from her lips smeared the cloth.

Music played in the background, a jolly man singing, "*Here comes Santa Claus.*" In the living room, logs crackled in the fireplace. Lights glowed on the Christmas tree. Colorfully wrapped presents lay under it. They only made the boy feel worse.

"Should I call the hospital?" he asked.

"The phones are broken."

"I can go down the street and try to find a pay phone, or ask a neighbor."

"Don't. I want you to stay close."

"But your cheek . . . "

"The ice is helping."

The boy frowned toward the nearly empty whiskey bottle on the counter.

"He promised."

"Yes," the woman said. "He promised." She took another deep breath. "Well . . ." She stood straighter, mustering determination. "We can't let him ruin our Christmas Eve. I'll . . ." She searched for an idea, but the look on her face told the boy she had trouble concentrating. "I'll make us some hot cocoa."

"Mom, you ought to sit down."

"I'm fine. All I need are some aspirins."

"Let *me* make the cocoa."

Still holding the ice pack to her cheek, she studied him.

"Yes, I don't know what I'd do without you." When she smiled, the effort hurt her injured cheek, and she winced again. She peered down. "My dress . . ." Its green had blood on it. "I'd better put on something else. Can't spend Christmas Eve looking like this."

The boy watched as she wavered into the living room, along the hallway, and into the bedroom on the left.

The music changed to "Frosty, the Snowman."

Cole limped into the living room and stared at the Christmas tree. He turned to the right toward the big picture window and peered out toward the falling snow.

Behind his eyeglasses, tears blurred what he saw. Nonetheless, he was able to distinguish the footprints in the snow where his father had crossed the front yard and opened the gate. The lane beyond the fence was deserted. The cheerless lights from the Christmas tree in the living room reflected off the inside of the window.

He promised, the boy thought. *He promised!*

ANDREI MOVED closer through the crowd, only ten people away now. The snowfall persisted, dimming the candles that burned in the paper bags along the street, deepening the shadows, providing cover. *Almost perfect*, he thought.

Music drifted from an art gallery, carolers singing, *"Oh, little town of Bethlehem."*

Again, Andrei heard the accented voice coming from the earbud under his watchman's cap. The Pakhan's angry tone was loud enough to hurt Andrei's eardrums. "We need to assume Pyotyr's a mole."

Pyotyr, Andrei thought bitterly. Of course, given what had happened, that surely wasn't the target's real name.

It was a measure of the Pakhan's anger that he'd stopped speaking in euphemisms. "The son of a *bliatz* probably belongs to law enforcement or American intelligence. But after everything we made him do to prove himself, I don't understand why he waited until *now* to make his move. Why *this* assignment?"

Maybe there were other times, Andrei thought. He recalled the failed missions and suddenly wondered if Pyotyr had been responsible for them.

The voice raged, "At least you found his cell phone. If help hasn't reached him by now, he probably doesn't have a way to send for it."

Yes, you're on your own, my friend, Andrei thought. *Ten more steps and I've got you.*

"This is *your* fault," the Pakhan's voice roared. "Make it right!"

Andrei thought back to when Pyotyr had arrived in Brighton Beach ten months earlier. Able to speak only Russian, the newcomer had kept to himself, earning money no one knew how. Always distrustful of outsiders, Andrei had followed him one night and watched as Pyotyr had used a pistol to rob a liquor store in the Bronx, beating a customer who resisted.

The next night, Andrei had seen him mug two drunks outside a bar in Queens. The night after that, he'd watched Pyotyr hold up an all-night convenience store in Brooklyn and pistol-whip a clerk so hard that blood spattered the window. Reporting this information to his Pakhan, Andrei had been ordered to warn the newcomer that he couldn't do any job without permission and that the Pakhan wanted a percentage.

Pyotyr had been furious, demanding to meet this all-powerful man who told everyone what to do.

"I worked away from the neighborhood. It's none of his business."

"It will be if the police follow you here."

"I don't make mistakes."

"Nice to meet someone who's perfect."

"Listen to me. I got along all my life on my own. I don't take orders from anybody."

"In that case, the Pakhan told me to kill you," Andrei said matter-of-factly.

"You can try."

"Very amusing."

"I mean it. Try. I won't let that yebanat *give me orders."*

"That's what I said when I first came to Brighton Beach. But I didn't have identity papers, and you don't, either. If I wanted to stay in the United States, I needed the Pakhan to help me, and that meant I needed to go along with whatever the Pakhan told me to do."

"There are other Russian communities where I can hide."

"And where other Pakhans enforce the same rules. You're willing to stand up to me. That's rare. So I'll give you some valuable advice— it's easier to do what he says than to force me to kill you. Save me the trouble. Take the jobs he hands out. You'll earn more than you do holding up liquor stores."

"Even after I pay him his cut?"

"Once he takes his cut and shows who's boss, he's generous enough to buy loyalty. Why else do you think I work for him? I don't like him any more than you do."

The Pakhan had tested Pyotyr on small jobs and found his ferocity to be so impressive that he'd begun pairing Andrei and Pyotyr on major assignments. For the past six months, the two had spent long hours in vehicles and alleys, had shared motel rooms, and had eaten more breakfasts together than Andrei had ever eaten with his wife. There was something about Pyotyr that impressed Andrei, perhaps because the younger man's determination and stubbornness reminded him of what he had been like at an earlier time.

In Colombia, if not for you, Pyotyr, that drug lord would have killed me.

What the hell happened tonight? Nobody turns against us. Viktor's dead because of you. The assignment's at risk because of you.

Damn it, I invited you into my home. I introduced you to my family. I trusted you when I never trusted anyone.

Be careful, Andrei warned himself. *Don't make this personal. That's how mistakes get made. I'll punish him. Yes, I'll punish him. But right now, he's just a target. Remember that, or he won't be the only one who's punished. Pyotyr doesn't matter. What's under his coat*—that's *what matters.*

A TEENAGER nestled a paper bag into a sling attached to a large balloon. A candle glowed inside the bag as the balloon was released and floated upward despite the snowfall.

Carolers sang, *"Oh, star of wonder . . . "*

Suddenly, a heavy man wearing a Santa Claus hat bumped against Kagan's left arm. The intense pain that shot through his wound almost made him groan. For an instant, he feared he was being attacked, but the clumsy man who'd knocked against him plodded on through the crowd. Still, it wouldn't be long before a real attacker reached him, Kagan knew. He sensed his hunters drawing closer, tightening the trap.

With a determined effort not to look frantic, he scanned the people in front of him and the gaily lit galleries on each side, his senses stretching wider. He shivered from the snow on his unprotected head and wished he could pull up the hood on his parka, but he didn't dare restrict his vision.

Can't risk missing a possible escape route, he thought. *Need to find cover.*

A lane appeared on the left, leading to a cluster of galleries, their Christmas lights haloed by the falling snow. Kagan kept moving forward. A street opened on the right, narrow like Canyon Road, almost as crowded, flanked by bonfires. Feeling the cold spread beneath the partially open zipper of his parka, he almost headed to the right.

The object under his coat squirmed.

No, Kagan decided. *That's not the street I want. We won't be safe there. We need to find another way.*

We.

The weight of the word struck him.

"Guide us to thy perfect light."

Wincing from the pain in his arm, he sheltered the baby under his parka and carried him through the snowfall.

"PAUL, YOUR FILE *says your parents became martial artists."*

"A substitute for gymnastics. Eventually, they earned black belts in karate. Given their fear of the Soviets, it was a good skill to develop. Of course, they never competed. Again, there was too much danger of publicity."

"Meanwhile, the State Department bought them a small house where they wanted to live, in Miami."

"Yes, sir. They moved there after taking an intensive English-language course. Even years later, they never quite got rid of their Russian accents. As a consequence, they seldom spoke to outsiders. If anyone asked where they came from, they used the cover story the State Department had invented for them and claimed they were the children of Russian immigrants.

"I can't imagine how foreign everything must have seemed to them, how confusing and terrifying, all because my mother wouldn't let the Soviets abort me. Think of it—they were only eighteen. Obviously, they couldn't afford to own the house we lived in, so they claimed they were renting it. If anyone asked why they'd married so young, they told a version of the truth and said that my mother had gotten pregnant before they were married, that they'd been forced to get married. Of course, they'd really wanted to get married, but putting it that way was embarrassing enough to make people stop asking personal questions.

"My parents had no skills, apart from gymnastics, so the State Department did the best it could and got my father a job at a landscaping company. When I was a baby, my mother stayed home with me during the day. At night, my father watched me while my mother cleaned offices."

"The American Dream. Paul, your file says that they took you with them to the martial-arts classes. You earned a black belt by the time you were fifteen."

"That's correct. Like my parents, I didn't compete. I didn't want the attention."

"A good instinct for a spy. How were you recruited?"

"The State Department maintained contact with my parents to make sure there weren't any problems. Evidently, its intelligence arm saw potential in me because I was good at sticking to the cover story and playing the role I'd been given."

"Why didn't your parents tell you the same lies they told everyone else? You'd never have known their real background. You wouldn't have been forced to play a role."

"They said they needed an extra set of eyes and ears to guard against threats. But I think they had another reason. I think they needed someone with whom they could share their secrets. It was a lonely life for them.

"My last year of high school, an intelligence officer came to our house and offered to pay all my expenses if I agreed to be educated at the Rocky Mountain Industrial Academy outside Fort Collins, Colorado. That was a big deal. My parents couldn't afford to send me to college. I was promised a job after I graduated."

"Was the recruiter forthright that this was an espionage school and that he was asking you to become an intelligence operative?"

"He couldn't have been more direct. His approach was that I could help stop the sort of repression that had caused my parents to live in terror, even after they came to the United States."

"An excellent pitch. I'm impressed."

"He was a first-rate recruiter. He understood how much I felt indebted to my parents. After all, they'd risked everything for me. It was a house of fear. I grew up hating the Soviets and any other group that made people feel as afraid as we did. The recruiter was right to approach me from that angle. He asked me if I wanted to get even. He asked me if I'd like to make a better world."

"So you went to the Rocky Mountain Industrial Academy. I taught there twenty years ago. That brings back a lot of memories."

"He promised I wouldn't be bored."

THE BOY STOOD at the living room window, watching the snow fall. Behind him, the music changed to "Jingle Bells," but the normally cheerful song only reinforced how empty he felt. As he took off his glasses and wiped his eyes, he heard footsteps behind him, his mother leaving the master bedroom and coming along the hallway to the living room. When he turned, he saw that her right hand continued to press the ice pack against her cheek.

She wore a red dress now. Its cloth was shiny and smooth-looking. The bottom part was long and spread out. Its red emphasized her blond hair and made him think of an angel ornament that hung on the Christmas tree.

"It looks very nice," he said.

"You're always a gentleman."

Limping, he followed her into the kitchen. For the cocoa, they heated rice milk instead of cow's milk because he couldn't digest the latter. There was just enough to fill two mugs. His mother put marshmallows on the steaming liquid.

"See, we can still have a party."

"I won't let him hurt you again," Cole vowed.

"Don't worry—he won't." She squeezed his hand. "I won't allow him a second chance to do it. We'll pack tonight and leave." She gave him a searching look. "Are you okay with that, with leaving your father?"

"I never want to see him again."

"Not the best Christmas, huh?"

"Who cares about Christmas?"

"I'm sorry." She peered down at the table and didn't speak for several seconds. "He has the car keys. We'll need to walk."

"I can do it."

"We could leave right now, but with Canyon Road blocked and so many people crowding the street, we won't be able to get a taxi." She looked at the smashed phone on the counter. "And we can't call for one, either. Canyon Road isn't open to traffic until after ten. That's when we'll set out. We'll find a pay phone somewhere. But even then, if the snow keeps falling, a lot of other people will want taxis. We might need to wait a long time. And since it's Christmas Eve, the hotels will be full. I don't know where we'll stay." She tried not to look at his short right leg. "Cole, are you sure you can manage a long walk?"

"I won't slow us down. I promise."

"I know you won't. You're the strongest son a mother could ever want."

IT ALL MAKES *sense now,* Andrei thought, advancing through the crowd, only eight people away from his target. The disguised containers of Soviet-era rocket launchers that customs officials managed to discover being smuggled through the Newark docks. The Middle Eastern visitors who were intercepted by the Coast Guard before they could be brought ashore one moonless night on Long Island.

Most assignments had gone as planned. There hadn't been any pattern to the failures. And Pyotyr had been so fierce on every job, doing whatever he was told—no matter how brutal—that no one had suspected him.

Certainly, I *didn't,* Andrei thought.

Although his waffle-soled boots were insulated, he felt cold seeping into them. But the discomfort was nothing compared to the frigid pain caused by the inferior snow boots he'd worn while on winter marches in the Russian army. *Our unit was Spetsnaz!* he thought with pride and bitterness. *Elite. We deserved better treatment.*

The snow fell harder.

Carolers sang, *"Away in a manger . . . "*

Focus, Andrei told himself. *Objectify. This isn't Pyotyr. This isn't the man who betrayed my friendship, the man I can't wait to punish. This is simply a target who needs to be eliminated.*

Moving nearer, he prepared to draw his sound-suppressed .22 pistol from beneath his ski jacket, to hold it low against his side, where the crowd wasn't likely to notice it. When he was close enough, he would raise his arm and place the suppressor's barrel near the soft spot behind Pyotyr's right ear. The small-caliber gun's report would be so muted, like a snapping sound from one of the bonfires at the side of the road, that even people nearby wouldn't react to it. The mushroom-type bullet would expand within Pyotyr's skull, bursting into fragments.

As Pyotyr fell, Andrei would seem to try to help him but would actually be grabbing the infant from beneath his parka.

His two teammates would block anyone who tried to interfere. In a rush, he would call for transport and use one of the few side streets to reach an area where traffic was allowed. Responding to his directions, a van would make its way through the snow to take him and the package out of the area.

Reflexes primed, Andrei followed the target through a four-way intersection. The next branching street was far ahead. Now the funnel truly began.

Despite his narrowly focused vision, even Andrei was aware that the most spectacular display on Canyon Road had come into view on the left. Dozens of tall trees bore lights and lanterns, the falling snow making them glisten. Past an open gate, evergreen shrubs twinkled with strings of bulbs that formed the outlines of giant candy canes, candles, and *Nutcracker* soldiers.

"It looks like a holiday card," a woman in the crowd marveled.

"Used to belong to Glenna Goodacre," another woman explained. "She designed the Vietnam Women's Memorial in Washington and the dollar coin that shows the Indian woman who helped Lewis and Clark."

"Her daughter modeled for Victoria's Secret, didn't she?" the first woman replied. "Married Harry Connick Jr."

Only five people separated Andrei from his objective.

Now, he thought, *while the crowd's distracted.*

Suddenly, a bearded man approached with two German shepherds. A boy reached out to pet one. The dog snapped at him. The boy's mother screamed. His father shouted.

People stopped to see what was happening. Others surged against Andrei, attracted by the commotion. Abruptly, the crowd became a wall.

Cursing, Andrei shoved through and encountered smoke from a bonfire. Shadowy figures moved beyond it.

Pyotyr! Where the hell are *you?*

KAGAN DIDN'T plan it.

Under his parka, he felt the baby kick. Adrenaline shot through him. At the same time, he heard a disturbance behind him, a dog growling, a woman screaming, a man shouting.

Again, the baby kicked. Harder. Sensing death on his heels, Kagan responded to an overwhelming impulse and charged ahead through the crowd.

"Buddy, watch where you're going!" a man yelled.

Smoke from a bonfire formed a thick haze that Kagan ran through, shoving people aside. He darted toward an opening on the right, trying to hide by hurrying along a walkway that led between galleries.

Ahead, a laughing woman stepped from a side door, a drink in her hand. Her eyes widened at the sight of Kagan charging toward her, about to slam into her. With a gasp, she spilled her cocktail glass and lurched back inside the gallery.

He sped into a courtyard, startling a man and woman who held gloved hands and admired a display of Santa's reindeer. The display was outlined by flickering lights. Surprised by Kagan's sudden arrival, the woman jerked back and almost fell onto Santa's sled.

"Hey!" the man shouted. "Watch it!"

Kagan spotted a lane that led straight from the rear of the gallery. As he raced down it, the snow fell colder and faster. Now that he was away from Canyon Road, he realized how noisy it had been—the countless overlapping conversations, the singing, the laughter, the crackle of the fires. In this less-traveled area, a hush enveloped him. Behind him, the lights of the galleries and the decorations became a faint glow.

All the while, he held the baby securely under his parka. On his right, a murky lamp over a garage provided enough light to show that other people had gone in this direction and trampled the snow. *Good*, he thought. *One set of footprints would attract attention, especially if they're widely spaced from someone running.*

He saw a shed and was tempted to hide behind it with the hope of ambushing his hunters. But there was too great a risk that he wouldn't see them in time to react. Hitting a target in the chaos of a gunfight was difficult enough during the day, let alone at night amid the falling snow. Plus, under the circumstances, how well could he shoot? Using his injured arm to try to hold the baby under his coat, he would need to fire one-handed. The cold might make him tremble, throwing off his aim. In addition, there were bound to be several targets. Could he hope to surprise all of them?

Yes, I've got plenty of reasons to keep going, he decided.

On his left, he saw a walkway that extended between low buildings. Feeling the baby kick again, he veered in that direction. But at once, he reached a wooden wall.

Frantic, he pawed along it and found a gap that was wide enough for him to squirm through. As he crawled, his knees felt the hard edge of a board under the snow. The moment he was safely on the other side, he raised the board and covered the hole.

Finding himself in a courtyard that was eerily lit by the city's ambient light, he studied the low adobe walls that surrounded him. A few snow-veiled lamps glowed in partially glimpsed houses. Hazy shrubs were strung with Christmas lights. The falling snow made the night seem blue, reflecting just enough illumination to reveal a few footprints that came from some of the houses.

Kagan kept moving. He reached a lane where he encountered yet another choice of which way to go. He had the impression of being in a maze.

The baby must have sensed his agitation. When he looked to the right, he felt it kick again, and he headed in that direction.

On each side of the lane, faintly glimpsed decorations glowed beyond fences made from upright wooden tree limbs wired to horizontal poles. From the Santa Fe newspaper, Kagan had learned that the locals called them coyote fences. In the old days, their purpose had been literally to keep out coyotes, and even today, coyotes were a common sight on the outskirts of town.

Kagan thought of predators. Hunters.

But it would take more than a fence to keep these particular hunters out.

"PAUL, WHAT DO *you know about Brighton Beach?"*

"It's next to Coney Island, in Brooklyn, sir. It's also the U.S. home of the Russian Mafia."

"That's correct. In 1917, a lot of Russians immigrated there to escape the Revolution. In the 1990s, so many more Russians went there after the Soviet Union collapsed that they started to call it Little Odessa. Quite a few were gangsters who used to belong to the KGB or the Soviet military, where they learned skills that make them especially dangerous.

"It's possible to romanticize Italian mobsters to the point that we think of them as Marlon Brando and Al Pacino in The Godfather. *But* Russian *gangsters are in a class of their own. 'Sociopathic' doesn't begin to describe them. They have no scruples, no shame, no code of honor. They'll do anything for money. There's no line they won't cross and no limit to their brutality.*

"An Italian gangster might suddenly feel patriotic and refuse if, say, Middle Eastern terrorists offered to pay to get a bunch of rocket launchers or a dirty bomb into the United States. But Russian mobsters'll take the money, do the job, and just get out of the way when the explosions start."

"COLE, WATCH the window," the boy's mother said. "Warn me if you see your father coming back."

Obeying, the boy stared into the semidarkness. Christmas lights outside the front door reflected off the snow and revealed that the lane was empty. He heard his mother pulling suitcases from under the bed in the master bedroom. He listened as she opened drawers and removed clothes.

Cole pushed his glasses closer to his eyes, working to keep his vision focused. Tension nauseated him. Even if he did see his father returning home, what good would *that* do? he wondered. He could shout to warn his mother. So what? The doors were locked, but his father had a key. In the end, they wouldn't be able to stop him from getting inside. How would his father react when he saw the suitcases filled with clothes?

I won't let him hit her again! Cole thought.

He limped to the rear of the living room and turned right to go down the hallway. At the end of the hall, he peered to the left, into the master bedroom, where his mother leaned over the bed. She was too busy packing to notice him. He turned to the right and entered his own bedroom, where he reached behind the door and gripped the baseball bat that his father had given him for his birthday in September. Not that the gift mattered. Lately, his father seldom found time to play with him.

Quiet, he returned to the living room, opened a closet next to the front door, and took out his coat. Its zipper made a clacking noise against the side of the closet.

"Cole?"

His fingers cramped on the coat.

"What is it, Mom?"

"The suitcases are packed. I'm a little more tired than I thought. We won't be able to leave for an hour or so, until cars are allowed on Canyon Road. I'm going to lie down."

"Are you okay?"

"I just need to rest. Let me know when it's ten o'clock. Or if you see him coming back."

Cole tightened his grip on the baseball bat.

"Don't worry, Mom. I'm here."

RAGING, ANDREI charged through the smoke of the snow-smothered fire. People gaped toward the commotion behind him. The second German shepherd was growling now, the boy crying, the parents and the dog owner arguing loudly.

The bystanders formed a wall that Andrei rammed through. He made no pretense of using his cell phone. If people thought he was talking to himself, it no longer mattered that he attracted attention.

"The target's gone!" he shouted into the microphone hidden under his ski jacket's zipper.

"Gone?" The accented voice bellowed through Andrei's earbud.

"The crowd shielded him! He ducked away!" Andrei stared furiously ahead, but he didn't see any disturbance in the crowd, no sign of anyone shoving people aside or rushing forward.

Pyotyr, where did you go? he thought urgently.

"The package!" the voice yelled. "Everything depends on getting it back! This is *your* fault! You vouched for him! You assured me I could trust him! You *hooyesos*, bring back what he stole!"

Andrei bristled. No one insulted him. From his earliest years on the streets of Grozny, he'd learned that disrespect could never be tolerated. If anybody other than the Pakhan had called him that . . .

Breathing quickly, he scanned the buildings on the left side of Canyon Road. They formed a wall. But to his right, several galleries had walkways between them. That was the only escape route.

His two teammates ran up behind him.

"Over there!" Andrei yelled, too hurried to recall the code names they'd been given. "Mikhail, take the first walkway! Yakov, take the second! I'll take the third!"

They rushed forward, ignoring the alarmed looks people gave them.

As the snow kept falling, Andrei raced along the third walkway. Christmas lights blinked in a gallery window. He passed a side door that was open, hearing a woman complain, ". . . almost knocked me over! What's the matter with people? This is the one night we ought to slow down. It's Christmas Eve, for God's sake."

Andrei ran into a back courtyard, where a man and woman stood in front of a flickering display of Santa's reindeer and sled. They looked angry about his intrusion, as if this wasn't the first time they'd been startled tonight.

"I'm with the police! Did a man run through here?"

"That way!" The woman pointed toward a lane. "Scared the hell out of us."

Andrei hurried into the lane. Behind him, muffled footsteps raced between the galleries, Mikhail and Yakov joining him.

"Those other routes are dead ends," Mikhail reported.

They assessed the lane. There wasn't much activity since most people preferred the attractions on Canyon Road.

Responding to their military background, they spread out. Andrei took the middle position and replaced his .22 Beretta with the powerful 10-millimeter Glock. He moved slowly, carefully, straining his eyes to study everything through the haze of the falling snow.

Yakov spoke in a low voice. "Too many footprints. We can't tell which are his."

"At least not yet," Andrei murmured, searching for blood.

"He might try to ambush us," Mikhail said.

"In that case, we've got him," Andrei replied. "The way we're spread out, he can't take all of us before we return fire. But I'm not worried about an ambush. He won't risk putting the child in danger, not while he still has strength to try to get it out of here."

Andrei was reminded of something a soldier, one of his mother's numerous boyfriends, had taught him when they'd gone on a hunting trip. The soldier had hoped the expedition would impress Andrei's mother. The soldier's unit was one of the first to be sent to Afghanistan in 1979, and Andrei had never seen him again. But because he and his mother had lived near a Soviet military base, there'd been many other soldiers to replace the man who'd left, and they were the only fathers Andrei had known.

Andrei had never forgotten that particular hunting trip. The soldier had taught him something that had turned out to be a life lesson. *A wounded animal keeps running until weakness forces it to go to ground. Only when it's cornered will it fight.*

IN WHAT SEEMED increasingly to be a labyrinth, Kagan plodded through the snowfall. Its muted whisper made him feel as if something were wrong with his hearing, as if he were trapped in a snow globe. Because he still couldn't risk

raising his hood and impairing his peripheral vision, he allowed the snow to accumulate on his head. Periodically, he
brushed it off. Nonetheless, his scalp felt frozen.

On the ground in front of him, the footprints were becoming less frequent, branching off to warm-looking homes
behind fences and walls. Soon, his would be the only footprints remaining. He prayed that the snow would fill them
before his hunters figured out which direction he'd taken.

As the baby squirmed under his parka, he shivered and
thought, *I risked my life for you. I could have walked away and disap-*
peared. God knows, I was ready. I've been through more than anyone
could imagine. I found terrorist threats no one would have dreamed of.

But to maintain my cover, I did things no one should have been
forced to do.

He thought of the clerk he'd pistol-whipped while robbing
an all-night convenience store in Brooklyn. His purpose had
been to demonstrate his ferocity to Andrei, who—he knew—
had followed him and was watching from across the street.

The clerk had spent two weeks in a hospital.

He thought of the restaurant owner whose front teeth he'd
pulled out with pliers, when the Pakhan had wanted the man
punished for failing to make a loan payment. Somehow, the
man's screams hadn't prevented Kagan from hearing the clatter of the teeth when he'd dropped them to the floor.

He thought of the legs he'd broken and the homes he'd
burned, the cars whose brakes he'd caused to fail and the water faucets he'd opened in the middle of the night, flooding
businesses whose owners had refused to pay protection
money. Again and again, he'd been compelled to prove him-

self to the Pakhan, to be increasingly brutal in order to gain admission to the inner circle and search for connections between Middle Eastern terrorists and the Russian mob.

He recalled how adamantly his mission controllers had refused to pull him out. There was always something bigger, something more dangerous that they needed him to pursue. They seemed determined to involve him in the mission forever, no matter how deeply he descended into hell.

Not any longer, Kagan mentally told the baby. *It's finished. I ended it because of you. Did I blow my cover because I wanted out or because you're worth the price?*

His weariness was such that, when the baby twisted against him, he almost believed it was assuring him that he'd done the right thing.

Lord help me, I hope so, he thought.

In the blue haze of the snowfall, he peered down and noticed that there was only one set of footprints ahead of him now.

Worse, they came in his direction.

And they were half full.

My tracks'll be obvious, he thought, feeling a deeper chill.

Suddenly, his dizziness from blood loss threw him off balance. Feeling the baby kick under his parka, he held it firmly with his good arm and jerked out his injured one to balance himself. He groaned from the pain but managed not to fall.

Rapid clouds of frosted breath came from his mouth. The cold mountain air made his tongue dry. He moved forward again, parallel to the footprints, hoping to make it appear that someone had left home to look at the decorations on Canyon

Road and had recently come back, that the two sets of prints belonged to the same person, leaving and returning.

Still dizzy, he reached a gate on his left. Beyond it, the faint footprints came from the side of a one-story adobe house. Its support beams projected from the flat roof in the manner of Native America pueblos. A covered porch stretched from one side of the house to the other. *But they don't call it a porch here*, a hotel clerk had told him. *It's called a—*

Stop losing focus! Kagan thought in dismay. His sense of being trapped in a snow globe had become so strong that it seemed as if the rest of the neighborhood no longer existed, that this house was the only place in the world. As he stared, it began to resemble a holiday postcard. A pine-bough wreath was on the front door. A row of colored lights hung above it. To the right, a window revealed a dark living room illuminated by a fire in a hearth and lights on a Christmas tree. He smelled the peppery fragrance of piñon smoke coming from the chimney.

The only house in the world? Don't I wish, he thought.

The baby moved under his parka, and Kagan wondered if it sensed how exhausted he was, that he would soon collapse, that this house was their only chance. He stepped closer to the upright cedar limbs of a coyote fence, straining to see if there was any movement in the shadows beyond the main window.

To the left, a light glowed behind another window, this one small. Kagan saw a suggestion of cupboards and concluded that the light was in the kitchen, but he still didn't notice any activity. The place seemed deserted.

Maybe the tracks belong to someone who lives here alone, Kagan thought. *Maybe he or she went for a walk and turned the kitchen light on to make it appear that the house is occupied.*

But misgivings made Kagan frown. Would someone have gone out and left a fire in the hearth? *It's not something I'd do,* he decided. *No, I can't assume the house is deserted.*

He directed his weary gaze farther to the left, where he saw a snow-obscured shed and a garage. *I can try to hide there,* he thought. *Maybe it'll appear as if the tracks belong to someone who returned to the side door of the house.* He glanced behind him, worried that his hunters would suddenly appear, phantoms racing through the snowfall, guns raised, overwhelming him.

Continuing to use his good arm to secure the baby under his parka, he reached his wounded one toward the gate's metal bolt. He bit his lip in a useless effort to distract himself from the pain. Then he tugged the bolt to the side and pushed the gate open.

"PAUL, YOU'LL SPEND *a month in a Russian prison in Omsk. That's in Siberia. The official records will indicate that you were a prisoner there for thirteen years. Russian prisons are notoriously overcrowded. The inmates seldom get a chance to mingle. It won't*

be suspicious if inquiries are made and none of the prisoners remembers how long you were really there.

"We'll put Russian prison tattoos on your chest. Barbed wire with thirteen prongs indicates the number of years you supposedly were in prison. A cat and a spider within a web indicate that you're a thief. A candlestick indicates that you're dangerous, that you're not afraid to put out someone's light. We'll give you a blood thinner before you're tattooed. The increased bleeding will make the tattoos look old and faded.

"We have a source who'll teach you details of Omsk at the time you supposedly were taken off the streets. Your story is that you're an orphan born there, a street kid who moved around a lot, running from the authorities until they put you in prison. Hard to disprove. A month in that prison ought to be enough for you to be able to answer questions about details only someone who served time there could know.

"After that, we've arranged for you to escape and take a black market route out of Russia. You'll make the traditional criminal pilgrimage to Brighton Beach, where you'll go through the inevitable rites of passage to be accepted.

"Paul, you've worked undercover before. The drill remains the same. The big difference is that this time you'll be doing it longer."

"And that the people I'm trying to fool are more dangerous. Exactly how much longer is the assignment?"

"We don't know. The rumors we're picking up indicate that something big is set to happen between the Russian mob and Al-Qaeda in the next twelve months. Maybe it's a suitcase bomb the mob took from one of those nuclear bases that were left unguarded when the Soviet Union collapsed. There's a strong chance you'll prevent an attack much worse than what happened on 9/11."

ANDREI'S RIGHT HAND felt cold. Its thin leather glove didn't provide enough insulation against the grip of his pistol. He pulled his left hand from his ski-jacket pocket, switched the Glock over to it, and shoved his right hand into the jacket, flexing his fingers, warming them.

In the dim illumination from snow-hazed lights, he and his companions followed prints in the snow. They came to a wall.

Andrei aimed to the right, toward a fence and the windowless side of a house. There wasn't any indication that someone had gone in that direction. He swung to the left toward a walkway between two rows of small buildings. A half-dozen sets of footprints led toward entrances. He hurried along, seeing the prints become fewer and fewer until only one set continued past the buildings.

I've almost got you, Andrei thought.

Abruptly, he came to another wall.

Inexplicably, the footprints didn't turn around. They just ended. Andrei stared at them, mystified. He stepped closer to the wall. It was made of upright boards that looked to be about ten feet high.

Pyotyr, you couldn't have climbed them, not with one arm wounded, not holding the baby under your coat. So where the hell did you go?

Baffled, Andrei stepped even closer and touched the surface. He exhaled quickly when a board fell away, revealing a low gap that was wide enough for a man to crawl through.

Clever. Are you waiting on the other side, ready to shoot us as we squirm into sight?

The Pakhan's voice blurted from the earbud under Andrei's cap. "*Have you found the package?* Our clients will be here any moment! Even if I give back the money, they'll demand someone be punished for failing to deliver what they need. It won't be me! They'll hunt you! I'll help them!"

Crouching, studying the gap in the wall, Andrei murmured to the microphone on his ski jacket. "We're close," he lied.

"You see Pyotyr?"

"It's too risky to talk. He'll hear me."

"You *govnosos*, get the package!"

Andrei felt the insult as he would a slap.

"Don't call me that."

"I'll do whatever I want, you incompetent *kachok*."

Andrei struggled to keep his fury from distracting him. Chest heaving, he stared toward the gap in the wall. He shifted to the right and left, using various angles to assess the area beyond. The footprints seemed to go straight ahead. But that didn't prove anything, Andrei knew. Pyotyr might have veered to the side and doubled back to ambush them as they crawled through.

We're wasting time. My friend, I won't let you make this even worse for me!

He reached under his ski jacket and pulled the radio transmitter from his belt. It was black plastic, the size of a deck of cards. He switched the dial to the frequency the team had used earlier and listened for some indication of what Pyotyr might be doing. What he heard was deep, fast, labored breathing, the sound of someone on the move.

Then you're not *waiting on the other side,* Andrei thought. *You made us suspect a trap—to make us stop while you kept going!*

Outraged, he squirmed through the gap.

As Mikhail and Yakov followed and spread out, Andrei examined his surroundings, keeping his gun ready. He was in a courtyard, with colorfully lit adobe houses on each side. Bending to examine the footprints, he noted that their stride wasn't as long. A hint of blood trailed next to them.

Pyotyr, we've almost got you.

He spoke into the microphone. "It doesn't need to be like this, my friend. Return the package. We'll forgive you."

Andrei's earbud was silent.

Then Pyotyr surprised him, replying, "Say it again, this time with conviction."

"Ah," Andrei said to the microphone, all the while following the footprints. "So you're not too injured to be able to speak. It's good to hear your voice."

"I bet," Pyotyr said, breathing hard.

"I meant what I told you. Return what you stole. We'll pretend this never happened. We'll even get you medical attention."

"And what about Viktor?" Pyotyr asked. "I killed him. You're willing to forget that?"

"He was new. I hardly spent any time with him."

"Your loyalty's touching."

"You have the *jaitsa* to talk to me about loyalty?"

"I made you look bad in front of the Pakhan. I apologize."

"Prove it. Return the package."

Pyotyr didn't answer. All Andrei heard was the sound of his forced breathing.

"You know we'll catch you," Andrei said.

"You can try."

"Listen to reason. You're losing strength. There's only one way this can end. Save yourself more pain. Surrender the child."

"And everything will be like it was before?"

"I'll let you go. You have my word."

"Of course." Pyotyr's labored breathing indicated that he kept walking.

"Damn it, tell me why the child is so important to you?" Andrei demanded. "If you're a spy, why would you blow your cover because of *this?*"

"It's Christmas Eve. I guess I got carried away by the holiday spirit."

"Is being sentimental worth your life?"

"Is chasing me worth *yours?*"

"I always liked your attitude, but given the way you sound, I doubt this'll be much of a contest."

Abruptly, Andrei came to a spot where the footprints joined a number of others in a lane that went to the right and left.

"Someone's coming," Yakov warned.

On the right, two couples emerged from the snowfall, prompting Andrei and his companions to tuck their weapons into their coats.

"No, you're wrong. Chevy Chase made the funniest Christmas movie," one of the approaching men insisted to his companions. *"National Lampoon's Christmas Vacation."*

"Is that the one where Chevy brings home a Christmas tree with a squirrel in it?"

"Yeah, and his dog drinks the water in the tree's dish. The tree gets so dry it bursts into flames."

"And burns the squirrel?" a woman objected. "You think that's funny?"

"No, it jumps on Chevy's back," the second man replied. "It's really just this cheesy stuffed squirrel that a prop guy sewed to his sweater, but his family screams and runs away when they see it on him. Then *Chevy* screams and runs, not realizing that the squirrel's on his back. And . . ."

Voices dwindling, the couples continued down the lane. Soon, their figures were obscured again by the falling snow.

Andrei and his companions removed their pistols from their coats.

"Pyotyr?" Andrei said into his microphone.

All he heard was forced breathing.

"We can solve this problem," Andrei assured him. "You just need to be reasonable."

Pyotyr refused to answer.

"Very well. I'll see you soon, my friend," Andrei said.

He switched the transmitter back to the frequency the team was now using. Then he put the unit under his ski jacket and rehooked it to his belt.

Mikhail pointed toward the ground.

"We need to hurry. All these tracks will soon be filled with snow."

Andrei glanced to the left, where this new lane led back toward Canyon Road.

"He might have rejoined the crowd," Yakov said.

"Possibly," Andrei agreed. "But he seems to be losing more blood. He might be afraid that someone will notice and cause a commotion that will tell us where he went. Would he risk attracting our attention instead of going to ground somewhere?"

Debating the possibilities, Andrei peered to the right, away from Canyon Road. There were fewer footprints headed in that direction.

"Go left. Check the crowd," he told Mikhail and Yakov. "I'll go *this* way."

KAGAN STEPPED through the open gate and studied the area in front of the house. As the snowflakes thickened, he saw the outline of a bench and an evergreen shrub on the right. Two leafless trees stood to his left. Their white trunks were difficult to distinguish in the snowfall. He stared at the main window but still didn't see any movement except for the flicker from logs in the fireplace.

At once, his vision wavered, almost in imitation of the dimly glimpsed flames.

It's just the snow blurring my eyes, he thought.

His legs felt frozen, as did his chest where the zipper on his parka was halfway down, providing air for the baby.

Hurry, he thought. He turned to close the gate and secure the metal bolt, ignoring a twinge of pain in his wound. When he redirected his attention toward the house, his vision again wavered.

Under his parka, the baby moved. Aware that he needed to find shelter soon, he took one step, then another. The flakes came faster, renewing the hope that his tracks would soon be filled.

I have a good chance of getting this trick to work, he thought. Still, he couldn't help imagining the emotions of the man to whom he'd spoken just now, the man he'd fooled into believing they were friends, the man who—even if he failed tonight—would never stop hunting him.

Kagan moved nearer to the house, but something he saw in the snow to the left of the front door made him worry that his vision had definitely been compromised.

He was sure he saw a plant. It had a dense cluster of dark leaves. The contrast against the snow was the reason he noticed it. But it seemed impossible. How could a plant grow in this weather? Moreover, it seemed to have flowers, a half-dozen large ones, the white of which was as difficult to distinguish as the trunks of the aspen trees.

And yet he was sure he saw their blur.

Flowers in winter? I'm hallucinating, Kagan thought. *Some kind of snow mirage.*

Or maybe the blood loss is making me see things.

Unsteady, he followed the half-filled prints toward the side of the house. *Keep going,* he thought. *I'm almost there. If I can get into the shed or the garage, I can rest for a while. Catch my breath. Try to stop the bleeding.*

He put one boot in front of the other.

Maybe there'll be a tarpaulin or an old blanket I can crawl under, he hoped. *Try to get warm. Try to warm both of us,* he silently promised the baby. He felt more responsible for the child than he'd ever felt for anyone else in the world. *Maybe I could wrap you up and put you someplace safe in a corner. That would give me a chance to try to protect us.*

But whatever you do, he mentally pleaded, *just don't cry. I'm sure you're hungry. I'll try to find you something to eat. I don't know how, but I'll do my best. Please don't cry. You've been good so far. The greatest. There's only one way you can be better. For God's sake, please don't cry.*

He shivered violently, wiping snow from the top of his head. He reached the side of the house. Away from the Christmas lights that stretched above the front door and the ceiling light that shone from the kitchen, he paused in the shadows, trying to let his untrustworthy eyes adjust. In the hiss of the falling snow, everything seemed closer, as if it were condensing around him.

Sudden movement dissolved the illusion. A figure lunged toward him, and Kagan was absolutely certain the shock from his wound had made him hallucinate—because the figure was a boy, maybe twelve years old, and the boy had a baseball bat. He was about to swing with it, and the intensity of the expression on his face was startling, even if Kagan saw it only for an instant.

His vision doubled. His knees bent.

Before the boy could strike him, he dropped. Sickened, feeling his eyes roll up and his mind drift, he did his best to topple onto his side, to keep the weight of his body from crushing the baby.

Don't cry, he silently pleaded. *Whatever you do, don't cry.*

But now the baby did cry. Jolted when Kagan landed, the infant wailed beneath the parka. Its cry went on and on, rising, pausing only when the baby took frantic breaths. Then it swelled again, a cry of helplessness and fear, of pain, hunger, and despair, of all the sorrow and desperation in the world.

"PAUL, YOU *shouldn't have risked calling. You're supposed to use the dead drop. Is this an emergency?"*

"I need you to bring me in. You told me it wouldn't last this long. Tonight . . . "

"I can barely hear you."

"Tonight, to prove I was part of the team, they forced me to . . . "

"*I still can't hear you. You need to get off the line. You're jeopardizing the mission.*"

"*If you don't bring me in, I'll walk away.*"

"*No. You'd make them suspicious. We'd never get another man in there. Give us time to think of a believable reason for you to disappear.*"

"*Soon. Think of it soon.*"

"*The quickest we can. Learn as much as possible. There are rumors about a shipment of plastic explosive being smuggled through the Jersey docks. That's Odessa territory. If Semtex is being smuggled in, the Russians are involved.*"

"*Just bring me home. For God's sake, bring me home.*"

Part Two

The Christmas Rose

KAGAN HEARD a faint choir singing, *"Silent night, holy night
. . . "* It took him a dazed moment to realize that the soft music came from a radio or a CD player, but not in the room
where he lay on his back on the floor.

A woman loomed over him, as did the boy who had nearly
struck him with the baseball bat. Kagan's eyes hurt from the
glare of the overhead light. Orienting himself in a panic, he
saw the gleam of stainless steel. A stove. A refrigerator.

I'm in a kitchen, he realized. He tried to raise himself, but
his strength gave out, and he sank back onto what felt like a
brick floor.

"You're hurt," the woman said. "Don't try to move."

"The baby," he murmured anxiously.

Even dazed, he was alarmed by the sound of his voice. For almost a year, he'd spoken so much Russian that his English had an accent. He worried that it would be one more thing to unsettle the woman.

"Here. I have him in my arms," she said.

The baby remained wrapped in a small blue blanket. Kagan's vision cleared enough for him to see the woman holding the infant protectively against her chest.

From his perspective on the floor, the ceiling light shone down through her long blond hair, giving her a halo. She was in her midthirties. *Thin, perhaps more than was healthy*, Kagan noted, desperation focusing his mind. His life depended on what he could learn about this woman in the next few minutes. She wore a red flared satin dress, as if for a party, although it hung askew on her shoulders, making him think she'd put it on hastily. And there was something wrong about her face, which she kept turned toward Kagan's left.

She stared at the crimson stain on the left sleeve of his parka.

"Why are you bleeding?" she asked. Her forehead creased with concern. "Why were you carrying the baby under your coat? Were you in an accident?"

"Turn off the lights."

"What?"

Kagan strained to minimize his accent. "The lights. Please . . . "

"Do they hurt your eyes?"

"Phone the police," Kagan managed to say.

"Yes. You need an ambulance." Holding the baby, the woman continued to tilt her face to Kagan's left, self-conscious about something.

What's wrong with her cheek? Kagan wondered.

"But I can't phone for help," she told him. "I'm sorry. The phones are broken."

While Kagan worked to order his thoughts, melting snow dripped from his hair. He realized that the zipper on his parka had been pulled almost completely open. Sweat from his exertion soaked his clothes. Heat drifted up from the bricks, a sensation that made him think he was delirious until he remembered a bellhop telling him about the under-floor radiant heating—hot water through rubber tubes—that warmed the hotel where he was staying.

"Broken?" He drew a breath. "The snow brought down the phone lines?"

"No. Not the lines. The phones are . . ." The woman kept her face to the side and didn't finish the sentence.

"Smashed," the boy said. Bitterness tightened his voice. He had a slight build, almost to the point of looking frail, but that hadn't stopped him from attacking Kagan with the baseball bat. He was around twelve years old, with glasses and tousled hair, blond like his mother's. Talking about the smashed phones made his cheeks red.

The baseball bat, Kagan abruptly realized. *Is he still holding it?* With relief, he saw that the boy had leaned the bat against a cupboard. Kagan didn't understand why the boy had attacked him, but there wasn't time for questions.

Dizzy, he tried to sit up. He remembered the microphone he wore. The woman or the boy might say something that would tell Andrei where he was hiding. Under the pretense of rubbing a sore muscle, he reached beneath his parka and turned off the transmitter. It was the first time since he'd taken the child that his hands had been free to do so.

To his left, he saw the small window over the kitchen sink.

"Please." He worked to neutralize the accent he'd acquired, his voice sounding more American. "You've got to pull the curtain over that window. Turn off the lights."

The baby squirmed in the woman's arms, kicking, crying again.

"Do it," Kagan urged. "Turn off the lights."

The woman and the boy stepped back, evidently worried that he might be delusional.

"As weak as I am, you can see I'm no threat to you."

"Threat?" The woman's eyes reacted to the word.

"Men are chasing me."

"What are you talking about?"

"They want the baby. You've got to turn off the lights so they can't see us."

"Some men are trying to kidnap this baby?" The woman's face registered shock. She held the infant closer, defending it now. The blue blanket was enveloped by the arms of her red dress.

Slow down, Kagan warned himself. *This is coming at her too fast. She needs time to adjust.*

He inhaled slowly, held his breath, then exhaled, each time counting to three as he would before a gunfight, working to calm himself.

Making his voice gentle, he asked, "What's your name?"

The woman looked surprised, unprepared for the change of tone. She hesitated, still keeping her face angled to the left. The baby whimpered in her arms, and its wizened face seemed to urge her to reply.

"Meredith," she finally said.

Thank God, Kagan thought. *She gave me something.* He noticed a night-light next to the stove across from him.

"If you're concerned about being in the dark with me, turn on that night-light. The glow won't attract attention from the street. It's the bright lights we need to worry about. Then I promise I'll explain why I'm injured, why I have the baby."

Meredith didn't respond.

"Listen to me." Kagan mustered the strength to keep talking. "I didn't intend to bring trouble to you. I planned to hide in the shed or the garage. Things didn't work out. I'm sorry I involved you, but that can't be changed now. Those men will do anything to get their hands on this baby. You've got to help me stop them from thinking he's here. That's the only way you and your son will get out of this."

If Meredith hadn't been holding the baby, Kagan was certain she'd have grabbed the boy and fled from the house. But the baby made all the difference, seeming to prevent her from moving.

"You can see how helpless I am," Kagan said. "What's the harm if you close the curtains over the sink and use the night-light? It won't hurt you, but it might save the baby."

Meredith kept hesitating, her strained features showing the confusion she felt.

"And it might save you and your son," Kagan emphasized. "You've got a known situation in here. A baby who needs help. A man who's injured. But you have no idea of the trouble outside."

When the baby whimpered again, Meredith looked down at its unhappy face and debated. She stroked its dark, wispy hair, then frowned toward the window.

Reluctantly, she told the boy, "Cole, do what he wants."

"But . . ."

"Do it," she said firmly, then added gently, "Please."

The boy looked at her, his gaze questioning, then moved toward the window.

"Thank you," she told him.

When Cole nodded, Kagan didn't bother trying to conceal his relief.

The boy surprised Kagan by limping slightly as he crossed the kitchen. He stretched nervously over the sink to close the curtains. Then he turned on the night-light, which had a perforated tin shield that looked like a Christmas tree and reduced the glow.

Watching Cole walk unevenly toward an archway that led into the living room, Kagan subdued a frown when he saw why the boy limped. One leg was shorter than the other. The heel on his right shoe rose two inches higher than the one on the left.

Even so, Kagan couldn't help silently urging the boy to hurry.

Cole flicked a switch on the wall and turned off the main kitchen lights. Apart from the glow of the night-light, the only illumination came from the fireplace and the lights on the Christmas tree in the living room.

Kagan allowed himself to hope.

"Okay, you said the phones in the house aren't working. But don't you have a cell phone?"

"No," Meredith answered uncomfortably. "Don't *you?*"

Kagan thought of the coat pocket that had been torn open when he'd escaped.

"Lost it."

"*He* took my mother's phone," Cole said.

"He?" Kagan crawled painfully toward a wooden chair at the kitchen table.

Neither of them answered. In another part of the house, a man's voice sang, *"Away in a manger, no crib for a bed . . . "* Kagan was surprised that he took the time to identify it as Bing Crosby's.

Damn it, concentrate, he thought.

"A man took your cell phone?" Kagan felt he'd achieved a small victory when his right hand touched the chair.

"You promised to tell us why they want the baby," Meredith demanded. "I made a mistake. I don't know why I brought you inside."

"You brought me inside because you heard the baby crying." Kagan fought for energy. "Because you couldn't leave the baby out there in the snow." He took a deep breath. "Because you're a decent person, and this is the one night of the year you can't refuse to take care of someone who's hurt."

With effort, Kagan pulled himself onto the chair. His gaze drifted toward a wall phone next to the night-light across from him.

At least, it had once been a phone. Someone had used a hammer to smash it into pieces. The hammer lay on the counter.

"Is the man who took your cell phone the same man who did *that?*" Kagan pointed toward the debris.

From his new position, he had a better view of the side of Meredith's face. Even in the dim illumination provided by the night-light, it was obvious that her cheek was bruised and her eye was swelling shut. She had dried blood on the side of her mouth.

"Is he the same man who beat you?" Kagan asked.

The question filled him with bitterness. To prove himself to the Russian mob, he'd been forced to beat many people. Often, the Pakhan had ordered him to punch women in the face, to knee them in the groin and knock them to the floor, kicking their legs and sides to make husbands, fathers, sons, and brothers do what the Pakhan wanted.

His mission controllers had been delighted by how effectively such tactics had earned Kagan access to the mob's inner circle.

But each night, Kagan had suffered nightmares—and each morning, he'd been filled with shame.

Now his shame reinforced his outrage at what had been done to Meredith. His powerful emotions started adrenaline flowing, giving him energy.

"If you don't tell me why those men want this baby, Cole and I are going for the police," Meredith threatened.

"No," Kagan blurted. "You don't dare go outside. It isn't safe."

The baby squirmed in Meredith's arms. Its tiny face shriveled and prompted Kagan to fear it was about to cry again.

"We can't let it make noise," he said. "It's hungry. You've got to feed it and change it. Can you do that? Can you help the baby? Anything to stop it from crying again."

The baby whimpered, pushing against Meredith.

"Cole," Kagan said urgently, "would you like to help your mother and me? Is there a bedroom that faces the front of the house? Does the bedroom have a television?"

The boy looked puzzled. "Mine."

"Go in there and turn on the television. Close the curtains but leave just enough space so the glow from the television can be seen through the window. We want them to think everything's normal in here."

Cole wrinkled his brow.

"Then go into the living room and look out the window. Pretend you're admiring the snowfall," Kagan told him. "If you see anyone out there, don't react. Just peer up as if you're waiting for Santa Claus."

"I'm too old to believe in Santa Claus."

"Of course. I don't know what I was thinking. Obviously, you're too old to believe in Santa Claus. Just fool anyone who might be watching. Admire the snowfall. Pretend you're a spy. Would you like to learn to be a spy?"

"Is that what you claim you are?" Meredith asked. Dismay crept into her voice.

"Yes." Kagan slumped on the chair, exhaustion overwhelming him. "God help me, yes, I'm a spy."

ANDREI FOLLOWED the various tracks along the lane, taking note as some of them angled toward houses behind chest-high walls, presumably evidence of someone returning home.

Or that's what I'm supposed to think, isn't that right, Pyotyr? Andrei decided. *But maybe one of these sets of tracks belongs to you.*

Solitary footprints went through a gate on the right. Andrei peered through the falling snow toward a living room window. Next to Christmas lights on a hearth, a man held up a treat while a Dalmatian looked up patiently and waited for its master to reward it.

Andrei returned the Glock to his right hand and put his left hand into a coat pocket, warming his fingers in the thin shooter's glove. He continued along the tracks, studying them, but he no longer saw with the tunnel vision of a hunter on the verge of catching his prey. His perspective was now wide, taking into account the trees and shadows to the right and left, on guard against an ambush. Earlier, with Mikhail and Yakov flanking him, he'd been confident that Pyotyr would keep running.

But with only me for a target? he wondered. *Pyotyr, will you take the chance of attacking me if I'm alone?*

Something flashed. The air became filled with an acrid smell.

Andrei spun, almost pulling the trigger as a burning object fell with the snow. At once, he realized that it was a plastic garbage bag shaped like a hot-air balloon. Inside, attached to an x-shaped platform of balsa, were rows of burning candles. The hot air they created had given the bag its lift. But not any longer. The candles had set the bag on fire.

When it crashed, sparks flew, the flames dwindling, smoke forming in the snow.

Andrei refused to allow the surreal event to distract him. He pivoted, aiming toward the shrouded area around him. Urgent questions crowded his mind.

Did it make sense for Pyotyr to go this way? Wounded? With the baby to concern him? Out here, away from the crowd, Pyotyr was helpless. If he fainted from blood loss, he and the baby would freeze to death.

Maybe I'm wrong, Andrei thought. *Maybe he believes he has a better chance among the people on Canyon Road.*

Or maybe that's what he wants me to think.

Andrei reached for the radio transmitter under his coat and switched the frequency to the one the team had used at the start of the mission, the one that had enabled him to speak to Pyotyr earlier. He hoped that the sound of Pyotyr's breathing would tell him whether or not he was still moving or whether he had stopped and set up an ambush.

But this time, there wasn't any sound. Only dead air.

Did you shut off your transmitter to keep the sounds you make from revealing where you are? Andrei wondered. *Well, it won't do you any good. I'll find you, my friend.*

He switched the transmitter to the new frequency the team was using. All the while, he scanned the hiding places that flanked the lane.

Ready with his pistol, he followed the dwindling tracks.

"THANK YOU *for inviting me to your home, Andrei. It's an honor to have dinner with your wife and daughters."*

"The honor is mine, Pyotyr. I owe you my life."

"But you'd have done the same for me. That's what friends are for—to watch each other's back."

"Yes. To watch each other's back. The Pakhan's other men ran. You're the only one who helped me out of that trap. And the bastard actually gave you hell for taking the risk. He gladly would have let me die to keep the rest of his men from being killed."

"Quite a life we chose."

"Chose, Pyotyr? Do you honestly believe we made a choice?"

"We stay here, don't we?"

"Where else would you go and not attract attention? With your fake identity card, do you think you could be an accountant or a real-estate agent in some place like Omaha? How long do you think it would take for government agents to show up at your door? But not before the Pakhan sent men to slit your throat to keep you from telling the government what you know about him."

"Believe me, Andrei, I wasn't complaining."

"Of course you weren't. Feel how cold it is. Look at the ice on the beach. The TV weatherman says we'll get another six inches of snow. Even then, I don't know why anybody grumbles. Brighton Beach is nothing compared to spending a winter in the Russian army."

"Or in a prison in Siberia. Perhaps we should go back inside and have dessert. Your wife'll think we don't like the oladi she made."

"In a moment. First we have business to discuss. That's why I asked you to come out to the porch."

"Why are you scowling, Andrei? Is something wrong? I swear I wasn't complaining."

"Hah—got you. I just wanted to make you worry so your surprise would be all the greater. I have very good news, my friend. You're being promoted."

"Promoted?"

"The Pakhan likes what I say about you, and what he's seen. He likes the intensity you bring to your work. He likes the results. Don't make plans for Christmas. You and I and some others, including the Pakhan, are going to Santa Fe."

"Where's that?"

"*New Mexico.*"

"*The desert? Good. I wouldn't mind a warm Christmas, drinking rum and Coke next to a swimming pool.*"

"*It's not the kind of desert you're thinking of, Pyotyr. This is high desert. Pine trees. Cold and probably snow. It's near a ski area in the Sangre de Cristo Mountains.*"

"*Sangre de Cristo?*"

"*I Googled the name. It's Spanish. It means 'Blood of Christ.' Apparently, that's what the explorers thought the sunset on the snow looked like.*"

"*Andrei, I don't understand why the Pakhan wants to go on a holiday where it's cold.*"

"*We're not going there for a holiday. We're going for a baby.*"

"A SPY?" Meredith's voice rose. "I should never have brought you into the house. Leave. *Get out.*"

"The baby. It's the baby you wanted to help."

"I made a terrible mistake. Go. If my husband finds you here when he comes back—"

"Is your husband the man who beat you?"

The question caught Meredith off guard.

Kagan turned toward Cole. "Is your father the man you wanted to hit with the baseball bat?"

In the glow of the night-light, Cole pushed his glasses onto the bridge of his nose. "I wasn't going to let him inside so he could hurt my mom again. The snow landed on my glasses. You were blurred. I didn't think anyone else would be coming."

"But you stopped when you realized I was a stranger."

"If you'd been him, I'd have used the baseball bat. I *swear* I'd have used the bat."

"I believe you would have." Kagan put his hand reassuringly on the boy's thin shoulder.

The baby started crying, rooting its mouth against Meredith's chest.

"Please," Kagan told Meredith, "do something. If the men outside hear him—"

"How do I know *you're* not the one who's dangerous?" she demanded.

Even though her attention was directed toward Kagan, she instinctively rocked the baby. Her raised voice made its tiny hands jerk with agitation.

"Do I look like I want to hurt you?" Kagan felt blood dripping from his arm onto the brick floor. He needed to take care of it soon before he lost so much blood that his strength was gone. "Do I look like I'm even *capable* of hurting you?"

"So much is happening. My husband . . . "

"Won't hit you again," Kagan said. "I promise."

That made an impression. Meredith became very still. Fixing her gaze on him, she no longer averted her face. Even in the dim light, it was obvious that her cheek was more purple, her eye more swollen than when Kagan had first seen her. The split at the side of her lip was larger than it had first appeared. But despite everything, he had a sense that she'd once been an attractive woman.

She's that thin because she's nervous, he realized.

"Won't hit me again?" Meredith's voice dropped. "I wish I could believe that."

"Hey, it's Christmas. Wishing will make it come true."

"If you do something to Ted, he'll only take it out on me later."

"That's his name? Ted? Don't worry. I won't do anything that would make him want to hurt you."

"Then how would you get him to stop?"

"Hey, don't you like surprise presents? Help the baby, and I promise Ted won't hit you again."

Kagan couldn't remember anyone staring at him harder.

"Somehow," she said, "you make me believe you."

The baby cried, kicking against Meredith's arms.

She reached under its blanket. "The diaper's soaked. But I don't have anything to . . . A dish towel," she realized. She held the baby with one hand and pulled two towels from a drawer. "Let's see if I remember how to do this."

She spread one of the towels on a counter and folded the other. Then she set the baby down on the first towel and eased its head onto the makeshift pillow of the second.

As she unzipped the baby's blue sleeper, Kagan saw that Cole still hadn't done what he'd asked. Again he urged the boy, "Go into your bedroom. Turn on the television. Go to the window in the living room. See if anybody's watching the house. If they are, fool them the way I told you."

"But what if somebody *is* watching the house?" Cole wondered. His eyes looked large behind his glasses.

"They won't try to get in right away. For one thing, they won't know for sure that I'm here."

"You think somebody's going to *break in?*" Cole's voice wavered.

Movement made Kagan turn toward Meredith. As she pulled the baby from its sleeper, the infant's legs curled toward its chest, emphasizing its vulnerability. Immediately, it jerked its arms and whimpered.

"They won't try to break in unless they hear crying," Kagan said.

"I'm doing the best I can," Meredith snapped. "With only this night-light, it's hard to see."

"No, that's not what I meant," he said in a hurry. "Please, I apologize."

"What?" Meredith looked at him in surprise.

"I guess I sounded disapproving. I didn't intend to. You probably get plenty of disapproval as it is. The baby can't ask for more than your best."

She studied him as if seeing him for the first time. Then the baby's squirming required her attention, and she tugged open the adhesive strips on the diaper.

Cole remained in the kitchen.

I've got to engage him, Kagan thought.

He unclipped the tiny microphone hidden under the ski-lift tickets on his parka. He put it deeply in one of his pants pockets, where the scratch of the smothering fabric would prevent it from transmitting voices. Then he removed his transmitter from under his coat and gave it to the boy.

"What's this?" Cole asked, curiosity mixing with suspicion.

Kagan took out his earbud, cleaned it on his pants, and handed it to him. "They're part of a two-way radio setup. That's the transmitter, and this is the earpiece. The on-off switch is at the top of the transmitter. The volume dial is on one side. The channel dial is on the other. Do you play video games?"

"Of course." Cole seemed puzzled by the question, as if he took it for granted that everyone played video games.

"Then you ought to be good at multitasking. While you watch for movement out the window, I want you to hold the receiver to your ear and listen while you keep changing the frequency on the transmitter. Maybe you'll find the channel the men outside are using. Maybe we can hear what they're planning."

Cole studied the objects in his hands.

"Make it seem like you're listening to an iPod," Kagan told him.

"Right. An iPod." The boy examined the equipment and nodded. "I can do that." He mustered his courage and limped into the living room.

Throughout their conversation, Kagan sensed that Meredith was watching him.

Then the baby squirmed, and she removed the diaper.

"A boy," she murmured. "He doesn't look more than four or five weeks old."

"Five weeks. Good guess," Kagan said. "If he'd waited a little longer, he'd have been a Christmas present."

Meredith dropped the diaper in a trash can under the sink.

"I forgot how tiny a baby is. Look. He has a birthmark on his left heel. It sort of reminds me of a rose."

"The child of peace."

"What?"

Kagan realized he'd said too much. "Isn't that what babies mean this time of year? Like the Christmas carol says, 'Peace on Earth, goodwill to men.' It's sexist, I suppose, but the sentiment still works."

Again Meredith studied him. Then she returned her attention to the baby.

"He isn't Anglo."

"Anglo?" Kagan asked.

"What the locals call 'white.' But he doesn't look Hispanic or Native American, either. His skin is like cinnamon. He looks—"

"Middle Eastern." Kagan stood and wavered. Managing to steady himself, he went to the kitchen sink and peered cautiously past the curtain on the window.

"I don't have any safety pins big enough to close this dish towel and make it work as a diaper," Meredith said.

Wincing, Kagan eased off his parka, freeing himself of the weight of the gun in his right pocket. When Meredith had opened the coat and taken out the baby, she hadn't pushed the flaps to each side and thus hadn't felt what was there. He set the parka on the kitchen table, taking care to cushion the impact of the gun against the wood and avoid a sound that might attract questions.

"Do you have any duct tape?" he asked.

"Duct tape? Yes, that would work instead of safety pins. But what made you think of *that?*"

"Duct tape has all kinds of uses. Where is it?"

"The bottom drawer, to the left of the sink. We had a leak under the drain."

Kagan opened the drawer and pulled out the roll of duct tape. He tore off two pieces and pressed them where Meredith held the folded dish towel around the baby's hips. Then he tore off several more strips—longer ones—and stuck them to the edge of the counter.

"For now, I won't need those," Meredith told him.

"They're for something else," Kagan said.

He turned his back, then unbuttoned his shirt and gently pulled it free. He didn't want Meredith to be alarmed by the Russian prison tattoos on his chest.

Despite the sweat that slicked his skin, he shivered. In the glow from the night-light, he managed to confirm that the bullet had passed through the flesh of his upper left arm. The wound was swollen, but as far as he could tell, neither bone nor the artery had been hit.

Well, that's the good news about the bad news, he thought.

He braced himself for what he needed to do. *You can manage this,* he told himself, fighting the pain.

Behind him, Meredith evidently got a look at the injury to his arm. "What happened to you?"

Kagan didn't answer.

"Is . . . ? My God, is that a bullet wound? Were you *shot?*"

"When I rescued the baby."

Repressing his dizziness, Kagan leaned over the sink and soaped the wound. "Do you have a first-aid kit?" He tried not to grimace when he rinsed blood away with warm water.

Meredith's mind seemed paralyzed. "A firstaid kit?" She was so overwhelmed that she appeared to have trouble understanding the concept. "Firstaid . . . ? The next drawer up."

Kagan pulled it from the drawer and opened it, pleased to find antibiotic cream. While he gingerly rubbed it over his wound, he looked through a crack in the curtains above the sink. The snow kept falling. He stared past the two trees toward the coyote fence and the lane. No one was in sight.

Maybe we'll get lucky, he thought.

Sure we will.

He noticed a dry cloth next to the sink. Biting his lip, he pressed it to his wound and used the strips of duct tape to stick it to his skin. Sweat beaded his face while he wrapped several layers of tape tightly around his arm, making a pressure bandage. He waited, hoping that he wouldn't see any blood leak out.

The baby whimpered. When Kagan looked over his shoulder, he saw it trying to suck one of its fists.

"What are we going to feed him?" Meredith said.

"Do you have any milk?"

"Babies aren't supposed to be fed regular milk."

"The World Health Organization has an emergency recipe for diluting it with water and adding sugar."

"We don't have any milk. Cole can't digest it. We had rice milk, but we used the last of it earlier."

"Then put a half teaspoon of salt into a quart of water."

"Salt?"

"Add a half teaspoon of baking soda and three tablespoons of sugar."

"Are you making this up?"

"It's something the Mayo Clinic developed."

Kagan shoved a finger into the bullet hole in his shirt. He tugged at the hole, ripping the sleeve open to make room for the added bulk of the pressure bandage. As he put on the shirt, he told Meredith, "Warm the water until the salt, baking soda, and sugar dissolve."

"World Health Organization? Mayo Clinic? Since when do spies know about feeding babies?"

"I once escorted a medical team in Somalia."

That was close enough to the truth to be believable, Kagan decided. The country had actually been Afghanistan, and he hadn't been an escort. Instead, his assignment had been to pretend to be part of the medical team while he tried to get information from Afghan villagers about the location of terrorist training camps. Knowing how to save a baby's life could buy a lot of cooperation.

"The babies were starving," Kagan explained. "The doctors told me what to do. It felt good to be able to help."

Reinforcing Kagan's point, Meredith held the baby against her chest.

"The mixture isn't a substitute for food. All it'll do is give him electrolytes and keep him from dehydrating," Kagan went on. "He needs twelve ounces in the next twelve hours. But after that, he's got to have formula."

Twelve hours, Kagan thought. *If we're not out of danger by then, it won't matter if the baby gets fed or not.*

"Someone's coming," Cole said from the living room.

WARY OF the shadows on either side, Andrei followed the tracks.

The falling snow had accumulated until it was above the ankles of his boots. The footprints ahead were rapidly becoming faint impressions.

Two sets veered toward a house on the right. Farther on, two other sets angled toward a house on the left. The pairs of prints were next to each other and showed no sign of scuffling. But Andrei suspected that if Pyotyr had used his gun to force someone to take him into a house, he would probably have done so with the gun pointed toward the person's back. In that case, one set of prints would be in front of the other. Also, the prints in front would be unevenly spaced, evidence that the person in front was being shoved.

As Andrei kept walking, faint light reflecting off the snow now revealed only one remaining set of fresh tracks. He noted that they paralleled some almost-filled prints that came in Andrei's direction, apparently from a house farther down the lane.

Do these fresh prints belong to you, Pyotyr? he hoped. *Have I almost caught you?*

Or maybe you're leading me into a trap.

Andrei slowed, scanning the snowy haze before him. The cold made his cheeks numb, but that only took his mind back again. While in the Russian army, he had once marched twenty-four hours in a blizzard. In that period, he hadn't been able to drink or eat anything, the weather having frozen his water and rations. *We do this to make you tougher*, his officers had told him.

Well, those bastards accomplished their goal, Andrei thought bitterly. *No one can be tougher or harder. Pyotyr, you're about to learn what that means.*

Ahead, the remaining footprints turned to the left toward the upright cedar limbs of a coyote fence. The prints reached a gate. Andrei carefully observed that the other tracks, the ones that were almost obliterated by the snow, came from that same gate.

They belong to someone who went to see the Christmas lights and then returned, Andrei concluded. The excitement of the hunt dimmed in his chest. *I've been following someone who lives in the neighborhood. I wasted valuable time. I should have stayed with Mikhail and Yakov and continued searching the area near Canyon Road.*

Wait. Don't jump to conclusions, he warned himself.

Continuing along the lane, he concentrated harder on the two sets of tracks. The old ones came from the left side of the house. The new ones went in that direction, disappearing into an area of darkness that Andrei assumed concealed a side door. Peering intently, he managed to see a shed and a garage over to the left. Switching his gaze toward the house itself, he noted that it had the distinctive architecture—flat roof, rounded corners, earth-colored stucco—that he'd seen almost everywhere in Santa Fe.

Christmas lights hung above a wreath on the front door. Immediately to the left, a pale light glowed behind a curtain over a small window in what was probably the kitchen. To the right of the door, a large window showed a living room, murky except for a dwindling fire in a hearth and lights on a Christmas tree. Farther to the right, in another room, a curtained window revealed the flickering illumination of what seemed to be a television.

Determined to be thorough, Andrei glanced toward the roof. The dim reflection of the front-door lights allowed him to see snow accumulating on a satellite dish.

He didn't study the house in an obvious way. Instead, his trained eyes took in everything as he walked past, seeming to admire the picturesque winter scene. The hiss of the snow almost muffled the sound of his footsteps. After twenty seconds, the house was no longer in sight, which also meant that he could no longer be seen from it.

With no more footprints to follow, there wasn't any point in continuing down the lane. Again, disappointment took hold of him. Stopping, he assessed the situation. His initial guess had probably been correct, he reluctantly decided. The tracks belonged to the same person.

But if someone had recently come back to the house, wouldn't there be more lights inside? Was it reasonable to believe that the person who lived there had gone to bed early on Christmas Eve, a night most Americans obsessed about because of gifts they were eager to receive?

What time is it?

Andrei pushed back the sleeve of his ski jacket and exposed the face on his digital watch. Obeying a habit from the military, he was careful to shield the watch with his hand before he pressed a button that caused its red numbers to glow. Quickly, he released the button and extinguished the glow.

The numbers showed 9:41.

If whoever lived in the house was elderly, it wouldn't be out of the question for him or her to go to bed early on Christmas Eve, Andrei decided. The flickering light from the television suggested that someone *was* in bed, perhaps watching one of those sugary holiday movies like *It's a Wonderful Life*, the title of which always made Andrei scoff.

A wonderful life? The only true parts of that movie were the old guy losing the bank's money and the rich guy wanting to control the bank so he could charge high interest rates and take people's homes. If the story had been true to life, the hero— what's his name? James Stewart—would have succeeded in killing himself when he jumped into the half-frozen river.

And why was he so damned skinny? Andrei thought. *Did he starve himself? Only in America, where there's so much food, do people starve themselves so they can be skinny. Go fight rebels in Chechnya on the half rations we were given. You'll soon change your mind about wanting to be skinny.*

Without warning, the Pakhan's angry voice shouted through the earbud under Andrei's watchman's cap.

"Did you find him?"

"Not yet," Andrei murmured into the microphone concealed on his jacket, keeping his voice as low as possible.

"When the clients learn we don't have what they paid for—"

"We're searching as hard as we can."

"If I'm forced to return the money, I swear I'll help them track you down."

"So you told me earlier. I haven't forgotten."

I've never been disloyal to you, Andrei thought. *I've always done more than you asked.*

"I just need a little extra time," he said into the microphone, concealing his bitterness.

"*Koshkayob*, you don't seem to grasp how little time you have."

Andrei's stomach hardened. He resented the insult as much as he hated being threatened—but nowhere near as much as he was furious that the Pakhan had chosen to support the outsiders against him.

"I can't talk any longer." Anger more than necessity made him end the transmission abruptly.

He turned and faced the snow-hazed lane along which he'd searched. As he went back the way he'd come, he knew he needed to hurry to rejoin Mikhail and Yakov, to search other places, to make up for the time he'd squandered.

But some instinct kept him from rushing.

The house appeared again, this time on his right. Again he studied it as he passed, moving closer so he'd be able to see through the gloom. The flickering light from the television. The Christmas-tree lights. The lessening flames in the fireplace. The coming and going footprints. The gate.

The gate.

There was something about it, something that nagged at him, but he couldn't decide what it was. He kept walking until once more he was out of sight from the house. He stopped, turned, and crouched, making sure his head was below the top of the fence.

He crept toward the gate, taking pains to stay down.

In his stooped position, the back of his neck was exposed to the chill of the falling snow. Nonetheless, he barely registered the sensation, so intent was he on the gate. He shifted closer, and the upright cedar limbs became larger before him. There was something about them. Something out of place. Something he couldn't leave without checking.

Reaching the gate, he sank to his knees in the snow. Ignoring the cold that seeped through his pants, he brought his face close to the gate and the bark on the limbs. He gazed up toward the snow that had accumulated on their sawed-off tops.

Some of the snow had fallen, dislodged by the motion of the gate. That was to be expected. Whoever had opened the gate might even have brushed against the snow on the top, causing more to fall off.

Brushed against the gate, Andrei thought.

He strained his eyes in the pale light that was reflected by the snowfall. The gate swung inward to the left. It wouldn't be unusual for someone's left side to brush against the gate when going through.

Concentrating, he found a dark smear near the bolt that secured the gate.

Excitement built in him. The smear was at the level of a man's arm. He had barely noticed it and almost dismissed it when he'd walked past, attributing it to a discoloration in the wood.

Now electricity seemed to shoot along his nerves when he touched a gloved finger to the smear and found that some of it stuck on the leather. Dark-colored, it was semisolid liquid, on its way to being frozen.

In the shadows, Andrei couldn't distinguish the color, but he had no doubt that this was blood.

"ISLAMIC TERRORISTS *thanked Allah when they found the Russian mob, Paul. In Middle Eastern countries, Al-Qaeda radicals don't look any different from the people around them, who just want to be allowed to lead their lives in peace. But if they leave their native countries and try conducting operations in the West, they stand out.*

"Before 9/11, they could move freely among us. We welcomed visitors. We were innocent. Now Middle Eastern terrorists know they'll be profiled if they do anything that's even the slightest bit unusual, so they need somebody else who can do the blood work for them, someone who blends.

"*Finding Westerners to cooperate with them used to be nearly impossible. After all, even the most callous criminal still has an instinct not to foul his nest. I'm not talking about love of country, Paul. That concept's too noble for the element we're talking about. But nearly everyone, no matter how corrupt, will refuse to do something that endangers his own tiny corner of the world— his neighborhood, his street, his house or apartment. It's basic self-preservation.*

"*Except for the Odessa Mafia, Paul. They're so detached from their adopted country that they don't even care about their homes. If they get paid enough to plant a dirty bomb in Manhattan, a bomb that's guaranteed to spread radioactive fallout to where they live in nearby Brighton Beach, they'll just pack up and move before they detonate the bomb. Pay them enough, and they'll do anything.*

"*And it's not only Al-Qaeda they'll work for. They're also taking money from Hamas.*"

"THERE'S A MAN outside the house," Cole said.

Kagan froze in the middle of buttoning his shirt. In the faint glow from the night-light, he doubted that he could be seen through the curtains that covered the kitchen window. Even so, he moved deeper into the room.

His normal pulse rate was sixty-five beats per minute. He now estimated that it was one hundred and ten and getting faster. Chest tight, he picked up his parka from the kitchen table and felt the reassuring weight of the gun in the right pocket.

He stopped at the archway that led into the living room.

"What do you see?"

"A man." Cole's voice was faint.

Only one? Kagan thought. *No, there'd be more.* Then the idea occurred to him that his hunters might have split up to cover more area.

Or maybe this is a false alarm.

"Cole, remember, don't seem to pay any attention to him. Just keep showing interest in the snowfall."

"I'm not at the window. He doesn't know I'm watching him."

"What do you mean?"

"I'm sitting in a chair that's away from the fireplace and the lights on the tree. It's dark here. He can't see me."

"You're sure?"

"Hey, I'm only a little kid. Nobody pays attention to a little kid, scrunched down in a chair. But I don't know how he could see me."

"What's he doing?"

"Just walking past. It's like he was looking at the Christmas lights and the snow. Now he's gone."

"Maybe he *is* just enjoying the lights and the snow. Could be he lives around here."

"We moved here at the start of the summer. I don't know all the neighbors, but I haven't seen him before."

"Maybe he's visiting someone. Describe him."

"I couldn't see him clearly. He's tall—I saw *that* much. Big shoulders. He has a cap pulled down over his ears. It's shaped like his head."

"It's called a watchman's cap." Kagan felt the shadow of death passing by. "What color is his coat?"

"It has snow on it, but I think it's dark."

"What about his cap? Is that dark, too?"

"It's got too much snow on it. I can't tell."

Don't let the boy sense what you're feeling, Kagan thought.

"That's the right thing to say, Cole. Always admit if you don't have an answer. A spy once wanted to keep his job so much that he told his bosses what they wanted to hear instead of the truth. It caused the world a lot of trouble. Which direction did the man come from?"

"The right."

From Canyon Road, Kagan thought.

Cole spoke again. "A dark—what did you call it—watchman's cap? Does one of the guys looking for you wear one? Wait a second. Here he comes again. From the left now. He's going back the way he came."

Kagan wanted desperately to step into the living room, to crouch and try to get a look through the window. But he didn't dare risk showing himself.

"He seems in a hurry this time," Cole said.

Kagan understood. Whoever was out there—almost certainly Andrei, given Cole's description—had followed all those footprints until the final set led him to this house. But Kagan's trick had worked, and Andrei had decided that the same person had made both sets, coming and going.

Now he's angry that he wasted time.

"He's gone again," Cole said.

"That's good. But keep watching."

In the background, Judy Garland sang, "Have Yourself a Merry Little Christmas." The only other sounds were the crackle of a log in the fireplace and the whimper of the baby.

Need to keep him from crying.

Careful to hide his tension, Kagan turned from the archway and faced the kitchen, where Meredith held the child.

"How's that mixture coming?" he asked.

Meredith stood a careful distance from a pot on the stove, holding the baby away from the flame.

"I'm heating it. But how do I feed him? I don't have a bottle with a nipple on it."

"Do you have a shot glass?"

"Somehow, I think I can find one." Her voice had an edge to it.

Kagan noticed that she frowned toward a whiskey bottle on the counter. The bottle was almost empty. A shot glass sat next to it.

"I see what you mean."

"I hope *you're* not going to start drinking," she said.

"Not to worry." Kagan took the glass and stayed to the side of the sink, away from the window, while he used hot water to rinse the alcohol from the glass. "A baby can sip from something small like this."

"No. When Cole was born, his pediatrician told me not to offer him a cup until he was four months old."

"Actually, a baby can sip from a tiny container soon after birth."

"You've got to be making this stuff up," Meredith said. "Do you really expect me to believe this is something else you learned from the World Health Organization?"

"It works. The trick is how you do it." Kagan went to her and pretended to put a hand behind the baby, demonstrating the technique. "Tilt him slightly back like this. Keep a hand behind his head to protect his neck. Hold the shot glass against his upper lip. Don't pour. That'll make him gag. If you let him control how much he sips, he'll do fine."

After a wary glance toward the window, Kagan went over to the stove and stirred the mixture, dissolving the sugar and salt. The spoon scraped against the pot.

"Cole, any sign of movement out there?" Despite Kagan's outward calm, he estimated that his pulse rate was now one hundred and twenty. His arteries felt the pressure that expanded them.

"No," the boy said.

"You're doing a good job. Keep watching."

The baby squirmed as if it might start crying.

Kagan quickly used the spoon to dribble some of the mixture on the inside of his wrist. "Slightly warm. It's ready." He turned off the stove and spooned the mixture into the shot glass. "I filled it to the one-ounce mark. We can measure how much the baby's drinking."

Meredith held the baby the way Kagan had shown her, protecting his neck from tilting too far back.

"Here we go, little fellow." She took the glass from Kagan. "Does he have a name?"

Kagan didn't reply.

"Sorry," she said. "I guess it's not something I should know."

"Actually, I was never told his name." Although Kagan's instinct was to avoid revealing information, in a way it no longer mattered. If the men outside got their hands on Meredith, the outcome would be brutally the same whether she knew anything about the baby or not.

He changed the subject.

"You're dressed like you were going to a party."

"The parents of a boy Cole goes to school with invited us to their house." Meredith sounded weighed down by thoughts of what might have been.

"Will you be missed?" Kagan asked quickly. "Will they wonder what happened to you? If they can't reach you on the phone, maybe they'll become concerned enough to—"

"Before Ted smashed the phones, he called them and claimed Cole was sick."

"Ah." Kagan's tone went flat. "Ted's a clever man."

"Yes. A clever man." Meredith took a deep breath and looked down at the baby. "I'd forgotten what it feels like to have something this helpless in my arms. That's right, little fellow. Keep sipping. I bet you're thirsty. Don't worry. We've got plenty, and it's all for you."

"Not quite," Kagan said. Dehydrated from bleeding, he was terribly aware of his own thirst. He reached into the firstaid kit, opened a container of Tylenol, and shoved four tablets into his dry mouth. Crouching to prevent his silhouette from showing at the window, he went back to the stove, tested the saucepan's handle to make sure he wouldn't burn himself, and poured some of the mixture into a glass he found next to the sink.

He took two deep swallows and got the pills down. He tasted the salt and the sugar. Instantly, his stomach cramped, aggravating the nausea produced by his wound. He waited, then took another swallow, feeling his mouth absorb the warm fluid.

"See anything, Cole?"

"It really looks like he went away," the boy said from the living room.

"Keep watching anyhow. It never hurts to be cautious. Spies can't take anything for granted."

"I keep changing the channel on the radio you gave me, but I don't hear anything. Maybe I'm not doing it right."

"If you play video games, I'm sure you can work that receiver." The microphone in Kagan's pants pocket was too far from his mouth to transmit his voice if Andrei happened to be listening on the frequency the team had first used. "Those men won't talk unless they need to. There's only a slight chance that you'll turn to the frequency they're using at the moment they happen to be talking. But we've got to try everything. You're doing fine."

Kagan switched off the night-light, noting that Meredith trusted him enough now that she didn't object. Concealed by the deeper shadows, he opened the curtains a couple of inches.

Through the falling snow, he was able to see the upright poles of the coyote fence. He watched for movement in the shadows beyond it.

"Meredith, describe the layout of the house."

ANDREI CRAWLED hurriedly through the snow along the bottom of the fence. His breathing quickened as the heat of the renewed hunt dissipated the cold on his cheeks. When he was far enough down the lane that he felt safe to stand, he did so and peered up at a utility pole.

Two wires led from it toward the house. In the faint reflection off the snow, he strained his eyes and saw that one of them was attached to an insulator on the pole—that was for electricity. The other wire was either for telephone service or for cable television. Then he remembered the satellite dish he'd seen on the roof and decided that the remaining wire must be for the phone.

In adequate conditions, his marksmanship was exceptional. But now it took him four shots before a bullet connected with the thick wire at the pole and blew it apart. Because of the falling snow, the sound suppressor on his gun was even more muffled than usual, and the sound of hitting the wire wasn't enough to attract attention.

Immediately, he removed the partly empty magazine, slid it into a pants pocket, and shoved a full fifteen-round magazine into the pistol. Only then did he speak to the microphone, his voice an urgent whisper.

"I found him."

Through the earbud under his cap, he heard an abrupt exhale.

"Thank God," the Pakhan's taut voice said.

Andrei thought it ironic that his leader, who had also been raised in the atheistic Soviet Union, would use that expression.

"Our clients are here now," the Pakhan said. "I've never seen anyone so furious. How soon can you deliver the package?"

"I don't know," Andrei answered.

"What?"

"Pyotyr took cover in a house. I need to figure how to get to him."

"Don't let him escape again," the Pakhan's voice warned.

"Not this time. He's ours."

"I don't give a *govno* about him! Deal with him quickly! The package! Just get me the package!"

It troubled Andrei that the Pakhan felt so threatened. Normally, he was content to provide barely adequate service. If clients complained, he ordered someone like Andrei to set fire to their homes. People who needed to employ the Odessa

Mafia were desperate to begin with. The Pakhan's attitude was that they ought to be grateful for any help they received.

But *these* clients were another matter.

The three million dollars they'd paid for a week's work— at a resort city, no less—had been too tempting for the Pakhan to resist. At the time, he'd called it easy pickings.

"They made all the arrangements. They bribed the necessary people. They learned the target's schedule, exactly when and where the job can be done. It should have been easy for them. But they can't carry out the actual mission. They need us because we can blend with the Santa Fe crowd, while they'd be spotted right away. So I charged those damned Arabs as much as possible."

Accustomed to causing fear rather than being the subject of it, the Pakhan now understood the penalty for going into business with clients who were even more ruthless than *he* was.

Andrei stepped off the lane toward a fir tree that provided a hidden vantage point from which he could watch the house.

"Did the rest of you hear?" he murmured to his microphone.

"Yes." Yakov's voice came through the earbud. "Where *are* you?"

"Follow the lane I took."

A few minutes later, when he saw two heavyset men hurrying through the falling snow, Andrei said to the microphone, "I'm to your right. By a fir tree."

The men paused, looking in his direction.

"There you are," Mikhail murmured. "Good. We wouldn't want to shoot you by mistake." Grinning at the joke, he and Yakov took cover behind the tree and assessed the house.

"How many people are inside?" Yakov's question could barely be heard.

"No way to tell," Andrei replied softly. "Someone walked off and made footprints earlier, but those are Pyotyr's footprints that go through the gate toward the house."

"How do you know?"

"Blood on the gate."

"Ah."

"There's light—probably from a television—in the room on the far right." Andrei pointed. "Maybe there's someone in the house, someone who isn't aware that Pyotyr snuck in. Or maybe the house is empty, and Pyotyr turned on the television to make it seem the place is occupied."

"A lot of maybes," Mikhail said. "He lost his cell phone. But if he's in there, he'll use the land line to call the police."

"I shot the telephone wire," Andrei told him.

"He could have phoned before you did that. Or maybe there's a cell phone in the house."

"Then why haven't the police arrived? Why don't we hear sirens?"

Yakov shrugged. "It's Christmas Eve on Canyon Road. The crowd would make it difficult for police cars to reach here."

"But we can't just leave or rush the house because we think the police *might* be coming," Andrei insisted. "If we screw up, we'd better run and keep running. We'd never be able to stop—because we know our clients and the Pakhan will never stop hunting us."

And my family, Andrei thought. *If the Pakhan can't find me, he'll go after my wife and daughters.*

"Then what do you suggest?" Mikhail wanted to know.

"We'll approach the house from three sides," Andrei decided. "Pyotyr can't defend it from every angle. At least two of us are bound to get in."

"Those are pretty good odds, as long as I'm not the one who gets shot," Yakov said.

"Pyotyr's wounded and weak from blood loss," Andrei countered. "His aim will be affected. There's a high probability that all of us will get out of this alive."

"'High probability' doesn't fill me with confidence. Whoever goes in from the front takes the greatest risk. How do we decide who—"

"The two of you sound like old women. I'll take the front," Andrei said irritably.

They stared at him.

"Pyotyr knows I'm the one he has the most reason to fear. I'll show myself in front of the house. He'll be distracted. That gives the two of you a better chance to get inside from different directions. If we synchronize the attack precisely—"

"We have company," Yakov warned.

Andrei pivoted toward the lane. At first, he worried that police were arriving. But the figure he saw was alone, plodding through the snow: a man wearing a buttoned pale-gray coat and a hat with built-in earflaps. He walked with his head so low that he looked weary.

The holiday blues? Andrei wondered. *Or maybe he's just protecting his face from the snow.*

A further thought occurred to him.

Maybe this is a policeman putting on some kind of act. If so, he won't be alone. He'll be setting up a trap.

Andrei thought of the Pakhan, of the clients, of Pyotyr.

Of his wife and daughters.

The man trudged closer, angling toward the opposite side of the lane, toward the gate.

I'll take the risk, Andrei decided.

"WE'RE GOING *to Santa Fe for a baby?"*

"Yes, Pyotyr. For the child of peace."

"I don't understand."

"Don't you read the newspapers? Don't you watch the news on television?"

"The news? Bah. Everything they tell us here is propaganda, the same as it was back in Russia."

"Then you've never heard of Ahmed Hassan?"

"Is that the child's name?"

"The father's. He's an obstetrician."

"Andrei, my English isn't . . . "

"Hassan delivers babies. He's a surgeon who once specialized in treating Palestinians who were shot in gunfights with Israelis.

Over the years, he operated on two thousand combat patients. 'But nothing got better,' he said. So he changed his specialty and became a baby doctor. Thousands of children are in the world because of him, far more than all the gunshot patients he treated. As he tells his followers, he chose life instead of death, hope instead of hate."

"His followers? You make Hassan sound like some kind of religious leader."

"In a way, he is. Although he doesn't have any religious authority, his speeches are so impassioned that a great many people are inspired by his sheer presence. He speaks like a prophet and attracts more disciples every day. They believe he has a vision. He preaches that war between Palestinians and Israelis will destroy the region and the rest of the world with it. Many—those who are tired of the decades of killing and destruction—agree with him.

"'The children,' Hassan reminds them. 'Think of our children. If we truly love them, if we treasure them as much as we claim to, we'll give them a future and create a lasting peace.'"

"Peace. You used that word to describe the baby."

"Yes, Pyotyr. The child of peace. Hassan's child. His enemies are paying us three million dollars to steal it for them."

"THE LAYOUT of the house?" Meredith sounded troubled. "Why do you need to know *that*?"

In the shadowy kitchen, Kagan saw her outline sit tensely straighter as she held the tiny glass to the baby's lips.

"No special reason," he answered. "Just a standard precaution. A way to fill the time."

"Precaution?"

"So I can anticipate."

"Anticipate what? You heard Cole. The man's gone."

"Probably. The thing is, it's always a good idea to have a backup plan."

In the meager light, Kagan couldn't see Meredith's eyes, but he was certain that she studied him nervously. The silhouette of her head nodded toward a dark archway next to a recessed side-by-side refrigerator-freezer at the back of the kitchen.

"The furnace and laundry room are through that arch," she said. "There's also a small bathroom, just a toilet and sink."

"Any windows back there?"

"No."

Kagan was grateful for that small blessing. "What about the rest of the house? Cole said his room is in front."

"Yes. In front there's the living room, a bathroom, and then Cole's room."

"What about in back?"

"Ted's office is behind the living room. The master bedroom is next to that."

"Across from Cole's room?"

"Yes. At the end of a hallway that divides that part of the house."

"How many outside doors do you have?"

Kagan noticed that Meredith's voice wavered as the logic behind his questions became impossible to ignore.

"Three. The front door, the side door here in the kitchen, and one through Ted's office. It leads to a back garden."

"What about an outside entrance to the basement?"

"There isn't a basement. Most Santa Fe houses are built on slabs."

Another thing not to worry about, Kagan thought. "Attic?"

"Not with the flat roof."

"The door in Ted's office, is it wood or sliding glass?"

"Wood."

At least they can't break through easily, Kagan thought. "Is it locked?"

"Yes. I checked it when I thought we were leaving the house to go to the party. Then I checked it again after Ted . . . left."

"What about the other doors?" Kagan went over and examined the one in the kitchen, confirming that it was secured.

"After Ted lost his temper, believe me, all the doors are locked."

Kagan took another wary look out the kitchen window.

"He wasn't always like this," Meredith said.

"How so?" Kagan encouraged her to keep talking in the hope that it would distract her.

"He knows he has a drinking problem. When we moved here from Los Angeles, he was determined to make a new start. In fact, that's why we came here. Last spring, he visited Santa Fe for a business conference. The night he returned, all he could talk about were the mountains and the light and how the air's so clean you can see forever. He kept saying the state's called the 'Land of Enchantment.' I understood. We definitely needed some magic."

"So you moved here?" Kagan prompted her.

"Two months later, in June, we were living in this house. On the Fourth of July, I remember, there was a pancake breakfast on the Plaza, thousands of people enjoying themselves. We sat under the trees and watched musicians playing bluegrass songs on the bandstand. People were dancing, having a wonderful time. Ted looked at me with a big smile and said, 'It's Independence Day, I promise.'

"Twice a week, he went to Alcoholics Anonymous meetings. We spent a lot of time as a family. We hiked in the ski basin. We drove across the valley to Los Alamos to see where they invented the atomic bomb. We explored the cliff ruins in Bandolier Canyon. Spanish Market, Indian Market, Fiesta. It was the best summer of my life.

"In September, Ted had some business pressures that stopped him from spending time with us. I didn't complain. The bills need to be paid. I did my part and got a job at one of the museums. At Thanksgiving, he brought home a bottle of wine. I must have looked upset because he said, 'Hey, it's not even red wine. It's *white*. It's nothing. I've been working seven days a week. What's a turkey dinner without a little white wine?'"

"And now, a month later . . ." Kagan said, letting his voice trail off.

"New location. Same old problems. I guess there's no such thing as a fresh start." After an awkward pause, Meredith changed the topic. "The baby's asleep." She set the glass on the kitchen table and carried the child through the dark archway next to the refrigerator-freezer.

Kagan heard her groping around back there and wondered what she was doing. Something scraped on the floor. Meredith's shadow reappeared. He saw her backing into the kitchen, dragging a wicker hamper.

"This was in the laundry room. I put towels inside it," she said. "It's almost as good as a crib." She set the baby in the hamper and covered him with one of the towels.

"In the laundry room, is there space in a corner behind the washer and dryer?" Kagan asked. "With room enough for you to crouch?"

"Yes." Meredith sounded puzzled.

"If something happens, take the baby and hide there. The metal on the appliances might protect you."

"Protect me from . . . ?"

Kagan turned toward the archway to the living room.

"Cole, are you listening?"

"Yes."

"Protect me from *bullets*?" Meredith asked.

"It's a bad idea for everyone to stay together," Kagan said. "That makes you all one target. Cole, if something happens, is there a place where you can hide?"

The boy was silent while he thought about it.

"There's a big television cabinet in here. I think I can squeeze into the space behind it." His voice was unsteady.

"If you're forced to do that, lie on the floor. You need to visualize what I want you to do. If you see it in your mind, if you rehearse it in your imagination and understand what you need to do, you won't be confused when the time comes. If something happens—"

"I'm not afraid."

"Good."

"I was scared when my dad hit my mom, but now . . . "

"Yes? Now?"

"I feel numb."

FROM HIS VANTAGE point behind the fir tree, Andrei watched the man plod through the falling snow. His shoulders were hunched. His head was down.

Within moments, the man was close enough for Andrei to conclude that his first impression had been correct—he looked weary, as if the weight of the world were on him. He glanced up only once, just enough to get his bearings and angle left toward the fence and the gate.

"Sir."

Andrei stepped from the shadows and intercepted the man before the two of them could be seen from the house. "I'm a police officer."

"Police?" The man looked startled. He was thin, about six feet tall. His hands were crammed into his coat pockets. The faint light reflecting off the snow made it difficult for Andrei to gauge the man's age any closer than midthirties. He had a mustache, an oval face, and a haggard expression. His breath smelled of whiskey, but not strongly. Any drinking he'd done had been a couple of hours earlier.

"What are the police doing here?" The man came out of his gloomy mood, straightening with concern.

"Do you live in that residence?" Andrei pointed.

"Yes, but—"

"What's your name, sir?"

"Brody. Ted Brody. What's this all about? What's going on?"

"There's been an incident in the neighborhood."

"Incident?"

"Do you know how many people are in your house, Mr. Brody?"

"My wife and son. Why do you ... My God, has something happened to them?"

"Mr. Brody, please just answer my questions. How old is your son?"

"Twelve, but—"

"Describe the house for me. Draw a diagram in the snow."

"Diagram? I don't understand."

"The rooms. The windows. The outside doors. That's very important. Show me the location of every outside door."

"Jesus, are you telling me someone broke in?" Brody pushed past, heading for the gate.

Andrei clamped a strong hand on his shoulder and tugged him back down the lane.

"Stop that. . . . I need to . . ." Brody struggled. "That *hurts.* Get your hand off me."

"Keep your voice down," Andrei warned. "You don't want to let him know we're out here."

"Him?"

Andrei hauled Brody farther back. "Don't raise your voice. We were chasing a fugitive. He entered your house before we could stop him."

"Then I need to get in there. I need to—"

Andrei stepped in front of him and grabbed both his shoulders. He spoke forcefully but at a low register, his face close to Brody's.

"Pay attention, Mr. Brody. If you go inside, you'll only give the fugitive another hostage. Don't put your family at greater risk."

"But—"

Andrei cut him off. "The best thing you can do is help us. Do you have a cell phone? If not, I'll lend you mine."

"Cell phone? Why?"

"There's a chance the fugitive doesn't know we followed him. I want you to call your wife and try to learn what's happening in there, what room she and your son are in, any details that might help the SWAT team when it gets here." Even though Andrei knew the phone line wasn't working, he needed to find out if there was a cell phone in the house.

"SWAT team?" Brody moaned. "Why did I let this happen? What have I done? I should never have left my family."

"Calm down, Mr. Brody. I'll rehearse the phone conversation with you. We need to assume that the fugitive will be lis-

tening when your wife talks on the phone. I'll teach you to
ask questions in a way that won't alarm him. We've got to
know where he is in the—"

"Wait a second." Brody stared past Andrei.

"What's wrong?"

"Those men over there. Who are *they*?" Brody pointed toward the fir tree.

"The other officers on the team. Detectives Hardy and
Grant."

Mikhail and Yakov each held up an arm in greeting, doing
their best to look like they belonged there.

"About the call you're going to make, it's very important that
you seem natural, that you don't let your voice indicate how
worried you are," Andrei explained. "The best thing to do is—"

"Don't bother. It's useless."

"Pardon me?"

"There's no point in calling."

"No point in—? But why?"

"The phones aren't working," Brody said.

Andrei felt his muscles tense. *Did he notice the telephone wire
I shot down?* He prompted Brody for more information.
"They're not working? What do you mean?"

"They're broken."

"You mean the snow broke the telephone lines?"

"No, I mean the *phones*." Brody seemed annoyed that Andrei couldn't grasp some obvious concept.

"Every phone in the house? How could they all be broken?"

Brody wiped snow off his mustache but didn't answer,
avoiding the question.

"Sir, we can't afford a delay," Andrei said. "The safety of your wife and son depends on you. *How* did the phones get broken?"

"I did it."

"What are you talking about?"

"I smashed the phones with a hammer." Brody sounded exasperated.

Andrei couldn't help expressing surprise. Just when he thought he'd heard everything, someone came up with something he could never have imagined. "Why on earth would you smash the phones?"

"So my wife couldn't call you."

"Call *me*?" Andrei shook his head in bafflement.

"You. The police." Brody stared down at his boots. "I lost my temper." The last word was tinged with despair. "My wife and I had an argument. I can't remember what it was about, probably my drinking. I . . . "

"But why were you afraid she'd call the police?"

"Because I hit her." Brody kept his gaze down. His shame made him whisper.

"Ah," Andrei said. So this wasn't something unimaginable, after all.

"It's the first time that ever happened. After I realized what I'd done, I spent the last couple of hours waiting to get sober enough to come back and beg her to forgive me." Brody suddenly looked up. "This is all my fault. If I hadn't left the house, I'd have been there when the guy broke in. I'd have been able to—"

"But don't you see? That gives you a natural excuse to call her."

"What do you mean?"

"You can tell her you're sorry and find out what's happening. It's so obvious an excuse, the fugitive won't be suspicious. Are you sure you smashed all the phones? Doesn't your wife have a cell phone?"

"I took it. Her phone's in my pocket."

"Does your son have a phone?"

"No."

Andrei tried not to show his elation. There wasn't any need to worry that Pyotyr might have been able to summon the police before the telephone line had been shot down. With no way to make a call, Pyotyr was completely isolated.

"Draw the diagram of the house."

"PYOTYR, HASSAN'S rivals tried to kill him several times. The last thing they want is peace. There's too much money to be made setting off car bombs in markets and sniping at Israeli soldiers on patrol.

"Paper bags of cash are distributed weekly from donations made around the world, millions collected from sympathizers who think this is about land or religion when it's also about men who have a very specific occupation—to cause violence and death. For decades, it's been the only profession they've known. If there were peace, where would their paper bags of cash come from? Even with Hassan's amazing effect on his followers, it's far from certain that he can achieve peace. Nonetheless, his rivals fear the astonishing growth of his influence and want to guarantee his failure.

"When he learned that his wife was pregnant, Hassan became so afraid for her safety that he sent her to the United States. Since July, she's lived secretly in Santa Fe, which has a small Muslim population loyal to Hassan's cause. In November, he made a secret trip here to monitor the last stages of her pregnancy and to deliver the baby. But he regretted sending his wife into hiding. He realized that he couldn't ask his followers to make sacrifices if he and his family weren't prepared to make them as well.

"As soon as the baby is strong enough to travel, Hassan plans to return to the Gaza Strip. He plans to stand in front of his followers and hold up his child as a symbol of hope. He plans to call it the child of peace and to say that every parent has a child of peace. His rivals want their weekly payments of cash so much that they'll do anything to stop him from gaining more sympathizers."

IN THE DARKNESS, Kagan searched a cupboard under the stove and found another pot. He filled it with water, put it on the stove, and turned on the gas burner.

"Why are you boiling water?" Meredith wanted to know. "There's still enough mixture for the baby."

"Sometimes, boiling water comes in handy."

"For what? Does your wound need cleaning again?"

"Do you have any tin foil?" he asked.

"Why would you need—" Looking baffled, Meredith gave up and pointed toward the left side of the stove. "The middle drawer."

Kagan opened the drawer, pulled out a box, tore off two pieces of tin foil, and crumpled them slightly.

"What about quick-drying glue?" he asked.

Despite her confusion, this time she didn't question him but merely said, "One drawer down."

"Thanks." Kagan pulled out the drawer and was pleased to find a large plastic tube of glue, almost full.

He went over to the microwave, which sat on the counter to the right of the stove. That counter was next to the kitchen's side door. He opened the microwave, put in the two crumpled pieces of tin foil, set the tube of glue between them, and adjusted the timer for two minutes.

"Wait," Meredith warned. "It isn't safe to start the microwave with those things inside."

"Just leave it like that. With the timer set." Kagan pivoted the microwave so that it faced the side door.

His parka lay on the counter. He took his gun from the right-hand pocket, the inside of which he'd partially sliced open to accommodate the sound suppressor on the end of his weapon.

Even in the shadows, it was obvious that Meredith stared. Kagan imagined how the gun appeared to her, the cylinder attached to the barrel making the weapon look grotesque.

"You had that with you all the time?" she asked.

"There didn't seem a right moment to tell you."

"You could have killed us whenever you wanted."

"The fact that I didn't threaten you with it ought to tell you there's a big difference between me and the men outside."

"If they're even out there any longer," Meredith said.

Kagan let her take refuge in that thought.

"I don't like guns," she told him.

"I'm not crazy about them, either, but on occasion, they can be helpful. In fact, we could use another one. Does your husband have a hunting rifle or a shotgun?"

"Ted's not a hunter."

"Some people keep a gun in the house in case of a break-in."

"Not us. No guns. Especially with Cole in the house." Meredith started to say something else. "And not with . . ."

Kagan imagined what she had almost said—*not with Ted's drinking problem.*

He reflexively reached toward the left pocket of his parka, but all he touched was torn fabric. He'd started the night with two spare ammunition magazines in there, but along with his cell phone, they'd fallen out when the pocket had been ripped open during his escape.

All I have is the ammunition in the pistol, he thought. *Fifteen rounds in the magazine, plus one in the chamber.*

Not much.

"Where are your aerosol cans?" he asked. "Window cleaner, furniture polish, anything like that."

Again, Meredith didn't ask questions. "The cupboard above the refrigerator."

Kagan opened the cupboard and took down four pressurized cans. He set two of them next to the kitchen door.

The baby whimpered.

Holding the two remaining cans, Kagan went over to the laundry hamper and peered down, tensely hoping the baby wouldn't start to cry.

"He's just dreaming," Meredith said.

"Babies dream?"

"Didn't the World Health Organization tell you about that?"

Kagan looked at her.

"Sorry," she said, averting her gaze.

"Humor's always welcome. It's good for morale." Again, Kagan peered down at the baby. "Weird how the mind plays tricks."

"Tricks?"

"On Canyon Road, when I was running from the men outside, the baby kicked me from time to time. I was light-headed enough that I almost had the sense he was guiding me, telling me which way to go, like he wanted me to come here."

"As you said, you were light-headed."

In the background, Rosemary Clooney sang, "I'll Be Home for Christmas."

Kagan drew a breath.

"Guess I'd better get to work." He shoved his gun under his belt, stooped, and crept into the living room.

The fireplace was on the left, its Southwestern design similar to one in the lobby of Kagan's hotel. The hearth was a foot off the floor. The firebox had an oval opening and curved sides. The flames in it had dwindled to embers, making it less likely that he'd be seen. His gun digging into his right side, he glanced to the right. In the middle of the shadowy room, a large leather chair faced the window.

"How are you managing, Cole?"

"It's hard staring at something this long." The boy's voice came from the other side of the chair's back. "I still can't get anything on the radio."

"You're doing a great job. I'll take your place soon."

The Christmas tree stood against the far wall. Staying low, Kagan went over and unplugged the lights.

It's late enough, he decided. *Turning off the tree won't seem unusual.*

The front door was to the right of the window. He crept over and made sure it was locked. Then he set the other two aerosol cans next to it.

He turned toward the rear of the living room. The Rosemary Clooney song came from an open door to the right of the fireplace. Inside an office, he found three computer monitors and keyboards on a table in front of him. Matching computer towers were under it. Despite the darkness, he had the impression of many shelves filled with electronics.

"Meredith, why is there so much equipment?"

"Ted designs websites for corporations. Sometimes he has three different layouts showing simultaneously."

Kagan felt a spark of hope.

"Then we can access the Internet. We can send e-mails to get help."

"No. Ted put an electronic lock on the Internet access. I don't have the password."

Kagan's excitement turned cold. "Ted thinks of everything."

He saw an iPod connected to a docking station and a set of speakers. That was the source of the music. Now Rosemary Clooney was singing that she might only be able to *dream* about going home for Christmas. When he turned off the speakers, the house became silent, except for the crackle of embers in the fireplace and the faint noise of the television in Cole's bedroom down the hallway.

At the back of the office, Kagan confirmed that the outside door was locked. The curtains were shut, concealing him as he shoved a table against the window. The table extended partway against the door and provided a barricade. His wounded arm aching, he picked up a chair and set it next to the monitors on the table. Intruders could break the window and get past the obstacles, but not quickly, not without making noise, and not without the risk of injuring themselves.

As Kagan worked, he couldn't keep from worrying that if Meredith still distrusted him, she might use this opportunity to take Cole and run from the house. At this moment, she and the boy might be opening the side door. He leaned from the office and glanced to the right, toward the kitchen, but Meredith's silhouette remained in view. She was looking down at the baby in the hamper.

Maybe she'll do it in a little while, he thought. *If I'm out of sight long enough, she might find the nerve to take the boy and run. And the baby—she'll probably take the baby.*

He could only pray that she wouldn't surrender to her fears and get all of them killed.

I COULD *do it now*, Meredith thought.

In the darkness of the kitchen, the only light came from the flame on the stove and the clock on the microwave oven. She thought of how the stranger had angled the microwave toward the side door, how he'd put two pieces of crumpled tin foil in there along with the tube of quick-drying glue. She still had a vivid mental image of the grotesque, long-barreled gun he'd shoved under his belt.

It made her shiver.

Table legs scraped in Ted's office. For some reason, the stranger was moving the furniture. *Blocking the window?* she wondered. *While he's busy, I can do this. I can get Cole. I can grab the baby. We can run. I don't know anything about this man. Maybe he stole the baby from its parents. Maybe the men looking for him are the police. Maybe whoever shot him was a policeman.*

I can do it, she repeated to herself. *I can do it now.*

Peering down at the baby, she imagined how she could go into the living room and put her finger over her lips to warn Cole to be quiet. She could motion for Cole to follow her. In a rush, she could pick up the baby, open the door, and run with Cole into the night.

There wouldn't be a chance to get coats. In the falling snow, she could hold the baby against her, using the blanket to shield him. She wouldn't be able to risk stopping to ask a neighbor for help. That might give the stranger time to catch them. She and Cole would need to run all the way to the crowd on Canyon Road.

We'd be safe there, she thought. *Can Cole run that far? Maybe we won't be able to move quickly enough.*

She wondered if the stranger would shoot. The thought made her flinch as she imagined the agony of a bullet slamming into her back. Or maybe she wouldn't feel anything. Maybe the bullet would kill her.

No, she decided. The one thing she knew for certain was that the baby was important to this man. The way he talked about it. The way he looked at it. He wouldn't do anything to put it in danger.

Did it seem logical, then, to think he was a kidnapper?

She heard him making other noises in Ted's office, cutting at something. But what? As the cutting sounds persisted, she thought, *Now's my chance.*

She took a step toward the living room, preparing to cross to where Cole watched the window, but then she remembered the way the man had looked at her and said, *"I promise Ted won't hit you again."* There'd been something about the steadiness of his eyes, the reassuring tone of his voice, the firmness of his expression—they'd convinced Meredith that he meant what he said.

"Don't you like surprise presents?" the man had asked. *"Help the baby, and I promise Ted won't hit you again."*

He hadn't said, *"Help me."* He'd said, *"Help the baby."* No, the man would never do anything to injure the baby, Meredith decided. *We can run without fearing he'll shoot.*

In Ted's office, the cutting sounds were now almost sawing sounds.

This is our chance! Meredith thought.

But what if he's telling the truth? What if there really are men out-side who'll do anything to get the baby? If Cole and I leave the house, we might run into them. I can't risk it. I can't put Cole's life in danger.

"I promise Ted won't hit you again."

As much as she was certain that the stranger meant to keep that promise, she was certain about something else. Because of Cole's short right leg, adults sometimes treated her son as if he wasn't smart or as if he wasn't even in the room with them. But the stranger had looked Cole directly in the eyes and had spoken to him as if he were much older than twelve. He'd trusted Cole to watch the window. He'd trusted him to listen for voices on the two-way radio. The respectful way he treated Cole left Meredith with no doubt that he would do everything in his power to make sure no one hurt her son.

KAGAN'S PISTOL wasn't the only weapon he carried.

On the outside of his right pants pocket, a black metal clip was hardly noticeable against the black fabric. The clip was attached to an Emerson folding knife concealed inside his pocket, an arrangement that made it easy for him to grip the knife without fumbling. When he pulled it out, a hook on the back of the blade was designed to catch on the edge of the pocket and swing the knife open. As he'd learned too well, there were numerous occasions when the ability to open a knife with only one hand could save his life.

He went over to a lamp on the office table, unplugged it, and pressed the blade against the electrical cord. He had no trouble slicing the rubber sheath, but the copper wires resisted, and he needed to press down hard, sawing more than cutting. He ignored the pain in his wounded arm from the effort of holding the wire against the table.

After he freed the cord, he tied it to the leg of a chair and stretched it calf-high across the office, securing it around a heavy box on the bottom of a shelf. Fortunately, the cord was dark. If an intruder broke through the window and shoved past the obstacles on the table, he'd be so fixated on the open door to the living room that he might not notice the trip cord in the shadows.

"Meredith, you said there was a back garden?"

When Kagan heard her voice in the kitchen, he was relieved to know that she'd remained in the house.

"A small one. The dry air at this altitude makes it difficult to grow things without a lot of water."

"Is the garden easy to get to? Are there gates to the side?"

"No. Someone could just walk around to the back."

"Or climb a neighbor's fence?" Kagan grasped at a thought. "Maybe the neighbors would notice a prowler and call the police."

"Not tonight," Meredith said. "For Christmas Eve, the family to the left is visiting a sick relative down in Albuquerque. The couple to the right loves to play blackjack. They went to one of the Indian casinos."

Kagan remembered driving north to Santa Fe from the big airport in Albuquerque. It had seemed that there was an Indian casino every twenty miles.

"The blackjack dealers are probably dressed as Santa Claus, but somehow I doubt the pit bosses think it's better to give than to receive," he said.

He hoped the attempt at a joke would help calm Meredith's nerves. Then his concern about the garden in back made him remember his hallucination when he approached the house.

"Meredith, I thought I saw a flower growing in the snow outside."

"You did see a flower."

"In winter?" Kagan worked to keep his tone casual, to relax her. "How's that possible? Why didn't it freeze?"

"It's called a Christmas rose."

"I never heard of it."

Feeling pressure in his temples, Kagan crouched, stepped from the office, and turned to the left, shifting along the hallway. He passed a bathroom on the right. Then, opposite Cole's room, he entered the master bedroom.

Despite the darkness, he managed to see two windows, one straight ahead above the bed, the other to the right of it. The curtains were closed.

Shadowy suitcases lay on the side of the bed.

"Planning to go somewhere?" Kagan asked.

"Away from my husband, as soon as Canyon Road was opened to traffic tonight."

"I bet you wish you'd gone earlier."

"Then I'd have missed all this Christmas Eve fun."

"Yeah, this is quite a party."

He set a chair on the bed, then put a side table and two lamps next to the suitcases, adding obstacles that might hold back someone who broke through the window above the bed. He pushed a high bureau in front of the other window, partially blocking the glass, making it difficult for someone to climb through. Next, he went to the remaining lamp, unplugged it, and sawed its electrical cord free. He attached it to the leg of a cabinet next to the door and stretched it across to a dressing table, rigging another trip cord.

In a bathroom off the bedroom, a night-light revealed a pressurized can of hairspray and another of shaving soap. Leaving the bedroom, he set the cans at the end of the corridor.

When he crept into Cole's room, a small television showed Bing Crosby crooning "White Christmas" to soldiers at an inn while a back wall opened and snow fell on a bridge across a stream. A horse-drawn sleigh went past. Everyone looked happy.

Kagan switched off the television.

Cole's room had only one window, facing the front of the house. Kagan pushed a bureau in front of it, but the bureau wasn't as tall as the one in the master bedroom, and he needed to put the television on top in order to block the window.

He rigged a third trip cord. Then he pulled drawers from Cole's bureau and set them along the bedroom floor. He took the drawers from the bureau in the master bedroom and did the same. He took the drawers from the dressing table and placed them along the hallway in an uneven pattern.

Kagan's gun dug harder into his side. As he crept back into the kitchen, the flame under the pot of water provided a minimal amount of light.

"You said it was a Christmas rose?" Approaching the limits of his strength, Kagan eased onto a chair and took several ragged breaths.

"Are you all right?" Meredith asked.

"Couldn't be better," he lied. "Tell me about the Christmas rose."

"You really want to know?"

"Believe me, I wouldn't ask if I didn't."

"Well, it's a type of evergreen," Meredith said.

Kagan nodded, encouraging her to continue.

"In Europe, some areas grow it easily in winter. It adjusts to the cold and often blooms around Christmastime. Clumps of large white flowers."

"Then I wasn't hallucinating."

"There's even a legend about it."

"Tell me."

"A little girl saw the gifts that the wise men had given the baby Jesus: gold, frankincense, and myrrh."

"And?" Kagan wanted to keep her talking.

"The little girl wept because she didn't have anything of her own to give. Then an angel appeared, brushed snow from the ground, and touched the exposed soil. The little girl noticed that where her tears had fallen, white flowers grew. Now she had something to give the baby: a Christmas rose."

Kagan gathered the energy to stand. Keeping a careful distance from the kitchen window, he looked for shadows moving in the falling snow.

"White flowers. That's what I saw."

"In Los Angeles, I liked to garden," Meredith continued. "I'd heard about Christmas roses, but I'd never been able to grow them. When we moved here, that new start I told you about was on my mind, and I decided to try again. A clerk at a local plant nursery said I was wasting my time because they're not suited for the thin, rocky soil we have here, but I guess I thought that if I could get one to grow, it would be a sign, something to show that Ted and I really had put our troubles behind us. Not exactly a miracle, but kind of, and the Christmas rose really did bloom. It . . . "

Meredith's voice dropped.

"I'm sorry," Kagan said.

"I guess it's just a stubborn flower. Tomorrow, Cole and I will move out." The significance of the word seemed to strike her. "Tomorrow."

Allow her to hope, Kagan thought. "In the morning, I'll help you."

AS SNOW kept falling, Brody bent forward and used a gloved finger to draw the diagram of the house. "Cole's room is in front on the right. There's a bathroom next to it." He indicated a door in a hallway. "Then there's the living room."

Andrei, Mikhail, and Yakov stood next to Brody, studying the shadowy lines in the snow.

"And in back?" Andrei prompted him.

"Master bedroom on the right," Brody said. "It has a bathroom you can reach only from the master bedroom. Then there's my office—in back of the living room."

"The kitchen's on the left as I face the house? What's behind it?" Andrei asked.

"A laundry room and another bathroom."

Lots of bathrooms, Andrei thought. Even after having lived in the United States for ten years, he still hadn't gotten used to all the bathrooms. When he was a boy, he and his mother had shared one with six other families.

"Show us where every window is."

Brody did so.

"In the back," Andrei said, "is there anything one of our team can stand on to look inside the house? He might be able to get a sense of what's happening in there."

Brody indicated the middle of the back of the house. "There's a brick patio with an overhang. We have a barbecue grill and a metal table with metal chairs. Someone could easily move a chair to a window and stand on it."

"Good. Now show us where every outside door is."

Brody added to the diagram. "When the SWAT team gets here, they're not just going to charge in, I hope. If there's shooting, Meredith and Cole might—"

"Don't worry. Our men are professionals. They don't shoot randomly. They make sure they've got the correct target, and even then, they don't shoot unless it's absolutely necessary."

"If anything happens to my wife and son . . . What did this guy do?"

"He held up a liquor store."

"You mean he's got a gun?"

"Please keep your voice down, Mr. Brody. Yes, we suspect he's armed."

Brody groaned. "If I hadn't lost my temper—if I hadn't left them alone . . ." A thought made him straighten. "Maybe he'll listen to reason. Maybe you can negotiate and stop this from getting out of control."

"That's hard to do without a phone. But there might be another possibility . . . "

Brody stepped toward him. "What?"

"It's risky."

"Tell me what it is."

"It could be that I was wrong," Andrei began.

"What do you mean? Wrong about what?"

"Not letting you go inside."

Brody shook his head in confusion. "But you said that if I went in there, I wouldn't do any good. I'd just become another hostage."

"That was before you told me the phones aren't working. We need to negotiate with him, and you're the perfect person for that. You've got every reason to walk up to the house. When your wife explains who you are, the gunman won't suspect you're working with us. Detective Hardy will equip you with a miniature microphone and earbud."

"Earbud?"

"A tiny earplug that works as a radio receiver. The microphone will allow us to hear everything you say in there, and maybe what the gunman says. Through the earbud, I'll be able to give you instructions."

"About what?"

"Things I want you to notice. By now, he probably rigged some kind of defense system. Booby traps. It would be natural for you to show surprise if you saw anything unusual. Your questions wouldn't arouse his suspicion. That'll give the SWAT team an idea of what to expect if they need to go in."

"Go in?" Brody looked alarmed again. "You mean they'll break down the doors and—"

"Maybe it won't come to that." Andrei spread his hands in a reassuring way, seeking to calm him. "You're a smart man. You might be able to persuade him to allow you and your family to leave."

Brody let the thought work on him.

"Yeah." He sounded hopeful. "I can try to make him listen to reason."

"Exactly."

"But what if he won't agree?"

"I always have a backup plan. In that case, if he won't let you and your family go, the microphone and the earbud will give me a chance to negotiate directly with him."

Brody seemed paralyzed by the dilemma. Finally, he asked, "You really think this can work?"

"The suspect has numerous arrests for robbery, but he's never shot anyone. I don't know why he'd be stupid enough to start now. There's a good chance to bring this to a successful conclusion. The question is, are you willing to do your best to save your wife and son?"

"My best to save them? Hell, I'm the reason they're in danger. If I hadn't gotten drunk and lost my temper, we'd all be having a good time at a party."

Andrei put a consoling hand on Brody's shoulder.

"Then maybe it's time to make things right."

"PYOTYR, THE DAY *after Christmas, Hassan, his wife, and his newborn son will use a private jet to fly back to the Middle East.*

"As a present to his wife, though—the last luxury she'll have for a long time—he's arranged for his family to spend four days in a suite at a hotel on Santa Fe's Plaza. The baby has three bodyguards and a nursemaid. With the child well protected, the wife will perhaps feel less nervous about leaving the hotel and going out to view the famed seasonal decorations in the city.

"Santa Fe is the capital of New Mexico. At eight P.M. on Christmas Eve, Hassan and his wife will be driven to a reception at the governor's mansion fifteen blocks away. There, amid numerous television cameras, he'll make an impassioned speech about his goals in the Middle East.

"Even though he's a Muslim, he'll use Christmas Eve to argue for mutual understanding and tolerance. He'll use his exceptional speaking ability to talk about the child of peace, who happens to be his son but who represents every Palestinian child. He'll tell the

world that he's taking the newborn baby back to the Middle East as a symbol of his hope for the future of all children in the region. He'll argue passionately that if people truly love their children, they'll do everything possible to demand a lasting truce.

"Pyotyr, what Hassan doesn't realize is that, although the infant's bodyguards are loyal, the nursemaid works for his rivals, who haven't the faintest interest in peace. All they want is to stay in the violence business that makes them so very much money—more than you or I could ever imagine.

"At 8:05 tomorrow evening, the nursemaid will free the dead bolts on two of the suite's doors. She'll tape a strip of plastic against the side of each door so that the latches can't seat themselves in the door frames and act as further locks. While Hassan and his wife are away at the governor's mansion, we'll enter the suite, shoot the guards, and grab the baby."

KAGAN GRIPPED the kitchen table and pushed himself to his feet.

"Cole, I'll take your place now."

He drank more of the mixture that Meredith had prepared, tasting the salt and the sugar. The now-tepid fluid trickled down his dry throat. His stomach absorbed it without the nausea he'd experienced earlier.

Just give me enough strength to keep functioning, he thought, not sure to whom he directed the words.

In the dark living room, he crept to the leather chair. When Cole's thin form slid away, Kagan eased into it, the leather creaking. He set the pistol on his lap, felt its comforting weight, and studied the window.

The Christmas lights over the wreath outside the front door illuminated some of the area. Beyond the two leafless trees, the coyote fence was vaguely visible, its waist-high cedar posts contrasting with the snow, but past it, the lane was hard to distinguish. If not for the threat that lurked out there, the view would have been comparable to what Kagan had noticed a little while ago on the television in Cole's room: Bing Crosby singing "White Christmas" while snow fell on a beautiful scene.

He suddenly realized that the boy had remained standing beside him. *Is he staring at the gun in my lap? Is it making him more afraid?*

"I need . . ." The boy sounded self-conscious. ". . . to go to the . . . "

Kagan relaxed slightly, thankful that the boy wasn't panicking because of the gun.

"Better use the toilet near the laundry room," he said. "I booby-trapped the hallway. It might be hard to get to those other bathrooms." Kagan couldn't remember when he'd last relieved his bladder. That he didn't feel pressure in it troubled him. His wound had dehydrated him more than he realized. "When you're finished, come back to the living room, okay?"

"You bet. The last thing I want is to be by myself."

"Bring your baseball bat. Hang on to it." Kagan noticed a big-screen television cabinet in the left front corner. Cole had referred to it earlier. "Keep imagining how you'll crawl behind that cabinet and stay low if anything happens."

"Maybe I won't need to," Cole said.

"That's what I'm hoping. Things are beginning to look in our favor. But as I said, spies never take anything for granted."

"It could be . . . "

"Could be what?"

"I don't think I want to be a spy," Cole said.

"At the moment, I don't want to be one, either." Kagan listened to the sound of the boy's uneven footsteps as he went across the brick floor and entered the kitchen. "Meredith?"

"Yes?" Her voice came softly through the archway.

"Please bring the baby in here and sit on the floor next to him. Be ready to rush him into the laundry room if you hear anyone trying to break into the house."

"If," she said. "But maybe they won't come."

"That's right. Maybe we'll have just a quiet Christmas Eve."

All the while Kagan spoke, he kept his gaze on the view beyond the window, concentrating on the fence and the lane.

He thought of the man out there with whom he'd pretended to have a friendship. *Did I fool you, Andrei? Are you searching for me near Canyon Road? When you don't find me, will you return here to take another look?*

I was a frequent guest in your home. Many times, I ate dinner with your wife and daughters. You invited me to help celebrate your wife's birthday. Once, when you were drunk, you called me "brother."

Even the guns we carry are identical: 10-millimeter Glocks that were part of a load of weapons the Pakhan sent us to pick up from a gun dealer in Maryland. We test-fired them at the dealer's range. We kept tying each other for the number of head shots we scored.

Because I betrayed you, because I made a fool of you, I know you'll never stop hunting me. If not tonight, then tomorrow or another day, you'll find me. That much I'm sure of.

Kagan remembered the many missions he and Andrei had conducted. With renewed self-loathing, he recalled the violence he'd been forced to inflict on his victims in order to win Andrei's confidence. Because of the secrets he'd learned and the plots he'd uncovered—missile launchers, plastic explosives, infectious materials, and other terrorist weapons being smuggled into the country—he'd saved many innocent lives.

But he couldn't shut out the memory of the clatter of the teeth he'd pulled from the restaurant owner and dropped on the floor, of the homes he'd burned, of the women he'd beaten while Andrei and the Pakhan had watched.

Meredith and Cole are as innocent as any of the other people I saved. They're in danger because of me. If anything happens to them . . .

Kagan's thoughts were interrupted by the flush of a toilet behind the kitchen. It sounded loud in the stillness. He heard Cole limp into the living room and sit on the floor next to the now-dark Christmas tree. The baseball bat scraped against the floor when he set it down.

"Do you like to play baseball, Cole?"

"I can't with this leg."

"Then why do you have the bat?"

"My dad gave it to me for my birthday. He hoped I'd grow enough that I might be able to adjust to my leg and play. After a while, he stopped trying. But I like to imagine."

A different scrape came from the wicker basket as Meredith pulled it into the living room and sat next to it. Kagan heard her settle against a wall. The baby made another whimpering noise and became silent again.

Good baby, Kagan thought. *Please don't cry.*

"Cole, I saw presents under the tree."

"I guess so."

"Is there anything special you're hoping for?"

"For my dad to stop drinking."

"Well, when we get out of this, I'll talk to him." The "when" was deliberately chosen, a projection into the future, a further way to make them optimistic.

"He won't listen," the boy said.

"You'd be surprised. I'm a very persuasive guy. When I mentioned the presents, I thought maybe there was something special that you'd like to open. This is a holiday, after all. What do you think, Meredith?"

She didn't respond for a moment.

"Yes, open something, Cole," she said quietly. "There's no reason to wait."

But Cole didn't reach for anything.

"Cole?" Kagan prompted.

"I guess I'm not in the mood."

"Sure. I understand. Well, if you change your mind . . . "

Despite the apprehension that coursed through him, Kagan's eyelids felt heavy. The exhaustion caused by his wound was taking its toll.

"Meredith, maybe you could make some coffee. Caffeinated, if you have it. With sugar. I can use the sugar."

He heard her crawl into the kitchen.

"Cole, did I see a crèche on a table next to the tree?"

"A crèche?"

"A manger scene. Little figures of Jesus, Mary, and Joseph. Donkeys, lambs, and other animals that would be in a stable. The shepherds."

"Yeah, there's one on that table," Cole said. "The three kings. You forgot to mention them. They're next to the shepherds."

"The three kings. Yes. I mustn't forget them. They're hardly mentioned in the gospels, but they're more important than most people realize."

In the dark, Kagan's fatigue settled over him. At the same time, his heart pounded at an unnerving rate, hammering in his ears, draining more energy. It was all he could do to stop his lungs from heaving in a desperate need to take in air ever deeper and faster, wearing him down further.

He used the gunfighter's rhythm of holding his breath for three counts, inhaling slowly for three counts, holding his breath for three counts, and exhaling slowly for three counts.

The irony was that he'd soon need the coffee he'd asked Meredith to make, that without a stimulant he'd eventually run out of adrenaline and crash.

Can't let Meredith and Cole know what's happening to my body. Need to keep distracting them, he thought.

The three kings.

His memory took him back fourteen years to the Rocky Mountain Industrial Academy, the covert espionage training facility he'd attended in the mountains outside Fort Collins,

Colorado. He was reminded of something he'd learned from one of his instructors, Robert McCaddam, a legendary spymaster who, according to rumor, had once been a Jesuit priest.

McCaddam, who was seventy-five at the time, enjoyed finding implications of espionage in all sorts of situations. Around Christmas, he was fond of standing next to a fireplace, lighting his pipe, and teaching what he called the true story of the season.

"Cole, I'd like to tell you a story. Will you listen? It'll put us in the Christmas spirit."

"What kind of story?" Cole sounded doubtful that *anything* could put him in the Christmas spirit.

"It's about the three kings." Kagan bit his lip to ignore the pain in his stiffening arm. "But the first thing you need to understand is, they weren't really kings."

"Then what were they?"

"You'll be surprised."

Part Three

The Magi

"IN THE NEW TESTAMENT, the only place the so-called three kings are mentioned is near the start of Matthew's gospel," Kagan said.

He stared out the window, looking for movement in the falling snow.

"Cole, did you ever read the nativity story in the Bible?"

The boy was silent.

"Or maybe you heard someone reading that part of Matthew's gospel out loud in church," Kagan suggested.

"I'm afraid it's been a long time since we went to church." In the kitchen, Meredith kept her voice low as she made coffee.

"Well, it can't be any longer than when *I* went to church last," Kagan replied.

That wasn't the truth—he said it only to keep bonding with them. That afternoon, he'd spent an hour in Santa Fe's cathedral, studying a manger display, his mind in a turmoil, trying to decide what to do.

"The reference to the so-called three kings is very small. Just a couple of dozen sentences. That's amazing when you consider how much has been written about them ever since. To understand what the kings really were, you need to realize that Matthew's gospel was written in either Hebrew or Greek. Over the years, it was translated into a lot of other languages. Changes crept in. In English, the word 'kings' didn't show up until centuries later. When language experts try to get a sense of the original words, the most likely translation is 'astrologers' or 'magi.'"

His mouth dry from stress and dehydration, Kagan listened to Meredith pouring water into a coffee-maker in the kitchen.

"To call them astrologers makes sense because they claimed to be following a star. But I prefer to call them Magi. Does that word sound familiar to you, Cole?"

"Not exactly."

"The words 'magic' and 'magician' are related to it."

As Kagan heard Cole breathe with the beginning of interest, he leaned forward, concentrating on something that seemed to shift in the haze beyond the fence, but he decided it was only his imagination. Or hoped it was.

"The gospel says they came from the east. If you look at a map and consider what was happening at that time, the country they likely came from was Persia. These days, it's called Iran. Have you heard of Iran, Cole?"

"Sometimes. When Mom and Dad watch the news on television."

"It's a country that's had a lot of influence on history. Today, there's plenty of tension and violence associated with it. Two thousand years ago, the situation wasn't much different.

"Basically, Persia wanted to control the area around it, and that included Israel, the country where Jesus would soon be born. The reason the Persians didn't invade Israel was that the Roman Empire claimed Israel as one of its territories. To attack Israel was the same as attacking Rome, and that was a bad idea. The Persians sometimes crossed the border and raided villages, trying to make Roman soldiers chase them—to lure them into an ambush. But the Persians didn't have the resources for an all-out assault, so they tried another tactic, the oldest and most reliable, much more effective than a battle: they sent in spies."

"Spies?" Cole asked.

Again, Kagan frowned toward what seemed to be a shadow moving within the snowfall, but the moment he focused on that area beyond the fence, the shadow dissolved like a mirage.

"The Magi were priests with tremendous political influence. The modern Iranian word for Magi would probably be 'ayatollahs.' That's a name you hear a lot in the news, although in ancient times the Magi were supposed to have secret, powerful knowledge that amounted to magic.

"Matthew's gospel doesn't mention a specific number of Magi who crossed into Israel. Traditionally, there are three because in the gospel they bring three gifts to the baby Jesus. Under the circumstances, it would have been foolish for more than three to go on this journey. The smaller the number, the better. They didn't dare attract attention."

Kagan smelled the coffee brewing in the kitchen. The aroma brought moisture to his mouth.

"Apart from the manger scene, Cole, what image comes to you when you think of the Magi?"

"Well, on TV or in drawings I've seen, they're on camels, and they're heading toward a big, bright star in the distance."

"Right. Some people theorize that it was actually a comet, or perhaps planets in a cluster, which happens sometimes, causing a brighter light than normal. Or perhaps it was an actual star, one that was exploding. Whatever it might have been, do you see any problem with trying to follow it?"

Cole considered the question. "The stars move."

"You're very observant."

"I never noticed when we lived in LA. There were so many streetlights that I couldn't see the sky. But here the sky's so clear, I can see all kinds of stars. My favorite constellation's Orion, the one with stars lined up like a sword. But at different times, he's in different places."

"Correct. Except for a few so-called fixed stars, one of which is the North Star, heavenly bodies shift across the horizon. In fact, the Magi probably used the North Star to guide their way across the desert. But they couldn't depend on a comet or a cluster of planets or an exploding star to show them the way because the bright light wouldn't have stayed in the same place all through the night. It would have drifted. At various times, it might have been overhead or even in the opposite direction from where they wanted to go. They'd have wandered in the desert until they died. Only a miracle could have kept the light in the same place and showed them the way. I'm not saying there couldn't have been a miracle, but that's not what this story's about. So the question is, Cole: the Magi must have had a different reason for crossing the desert at night. What do you think it was?"

"To avoid the heat of the day."

"Good answer."

"But in school, we've been studying weather patterns, ice ages and stuff like that, to learn if climate change is real or not. Our teacher says that back then, some deserts might not have been as hot as they are now."

"I read the same thing." Kagan concentrated on the snow falling beyond the window. "So let's suppose traveling across the desert in daylight wouldn't have been as dangerous as it is now. What's another reason the Magi would have wanted to travel at night? On camels. For at least a month. It would have been difficult to keep the camels from stumbling in the dark and breaking their legs. That definitely would have been dangerous. So what's the advantage of the night?"

Cole didn't have an answer.

"Suppose this is a war story," Kagan suggested.

"Maybe they were trying to keep the Roman soldiers from seeing them?"

"Cole, you should think twice about not wanting to be a spy. You're right. The Magi traveled in the dark because they were on a secret mission and they didn't want the soldiers to see them."

"THE MICROPHONE has a pin on the back," Andrei said. "I attached it under your coat collar. It's set so you're broadcasting all the time. I'll hear everything you say and most of what's said around you. On occasion, I'll give you instructions through this earbud."

Andrei placed the device in Brody's left ear.

"But won't the gunman see it?" Brody's voice was unsteady, from more than just the cold.

"Keep your hat on and your earflaps down as long as possible. Eventually, you'll need to take the hat off, but the earbud's small and flesh-colored: hard to see, even in the daytime. He's got the lights off. I guarantee he won't turn them on."

"Even the Christmastree lights and the television are off now," Mikhail said, watching the house from the cover of the fir tree.

"The microphone and the earbud have tiny batteries," Andrei told Brody. "They're boosted by this transmitter/

receiver you'd normally wear on your belt. But if the suspect searches you—which I assume he will—he's bound to find it, even in the dark, so we need to hide it on you. The best place is in one of your gloves. Take them off as you approach the house. Set them someplace as soon as you're inside.

"I dialed your equipment to its own channel. That way, you won't be distracted when I talk to headquarters. Now, let's find out if everything works. Detective Grant, walk down the lane and say something into your microphone."

As Yakov left them, Andrei heard a voice through his own earbud, but it didn't belong to Yakov.

The Pakhan's voice was sharp. "Our clients believe I took their money without any intention of delivering the package! They insist I'm lying! They claim I'm planning to sell the baby to someone else!"

In the background, something crashed. A man with an Arab accent shouted, "Would you like me to cut off your thumbs? Your ears?"

"Your balls!" another accented voice threatened. "We'll make you eat them! That's what we do to people who cheat us!"

Andrei looked at Brody but gave no sign of what he was hearing. "I have a call coming through. Excuse me."

Because Brody knew about the microphones, it wasn't necessary to go through the charade of pretending to talk to a cell phone, as Andrei had done earlier among the crowd on Canyon Road. But now he had a different reason for pretending to use his cell phone.

He took it from a pocket and opened it. At once, he intentionally fumbled with it and let it fall into the snow.

"Damn."

Continuing the pretense, he pawed in the snow. His thin leather glove barely protected his fingers from the cold. When he found the phone, it was covered with flakes. He wiped them off, made a show of pressing a button, and frowned at the screen.

"Something's wrong."

"Your phone doesn't work?" Brody asked.

"Snow must have got into it. Here, lend me yours."

When Brody handed it over, Andrei pressed numbers and walked a short distance away, pretending to talk on the phone while he actually spoke to the microphone on his ski jacket.

"Did you just try to call me?"

"What was *that* about?" the Pakhan demanded through Andrei's earbud. He sounded furious.

"Something I needed to do. I'll explain later."

"Did you hear what I said? Our clients claim I cheated them! But I won't take the blame because you screwed up! I'll make sure they know who to punish!"

Andrei barely held his anger in check. "Tell them they'll get the package before midnight."

"You guarantee that?"

"When we deliver, demand a bonus."

"Answer me! *Do you guarantee delivery?*"

In the cold, Andrei's cheeks felt hot. Somehow he managed to keep his voice low and maintain control. Almost.

"Damn it, yes. Now let me do my work."

With that, he pretended to shut off the phone.

"What's the matter?" Brody asked.

"You've got family problems. So do I."

Down the lane, Andrei heard Yakov murmur, "Testing. One, two, three, four."

In response, Brody pressed a finger to the object in his left ear. "I hear him."

When Yakov returned, Andrei asked, "Detective Grant, is Mr. Brody's microphone working? Did his voice come through your earbud?"

"Clearly."

"Excellent." Amid the distraction, Andrei slipped Brody's cell phone into his pocket.

Brody didn't notice.

"Okay," Andrei said. "Now, let's practice what you're going to do."

SNOW CLUNG to their coats as they left the stairwell, passed the elevator, and walked along a hotel corridor to the security door.

There were five of them—Andrei, Kagan, Yakov, Mikhail, and Viktor, a lanky man Kagan had met only a half-dozen times, newly *arrived from Russia. Andrei slid a credit-card-shaped hotel key into a slot. Making a slight metallic sound, the lock electronically opened.*

Andrei wore his leather shooter's gloves so he wouldn't leave fingerprints when he turned the doorknob. Coordinating their movements via their earbuds and hidden microphones, he and the others had gone into the hotel through separate entrances to avoid attracting attention. They'd lowered their heads when passing security cameras. They did the same now as they stepped under the last camera they needed to be concerned about.

Closing the door, they entered a continuation of the corridor. Numbered rooms stretched along the wall to the left. In this exclusive part of the hotel, an attractive, well-dressed female receptionist smiled at them from a desk and pointed toward the melting flakes on their coats. "I see it hasn't stopped snowing."

"A picturesque night for a walk," Andrei replied.

"Have you been to Canyon Road?" the red-haired woman asked.

"Very impressive."

"It's the big attraction on Christmas Eve. All year-round, in fact. I'm glad you didn't miss it. Is there anything I can get you?"

"Thank you, no."

"You must have checked into the hotel when I wasn't on duty. I don't recall seeing you before."

"I don't recall seeing you, either. We only came back to our rooms to pick up some presents we're taking to a party."

"Have a good time."

"We intend to."

As expected on Christmas Eve, no sounds came from any of the rooms, the guests having gone out to dinner, to enjoy the sights, or perhaps to attend mass in the nearby cathedral. But even though there was virtually no risk of being interrupted, speed was essential.

While Andrei spoke to the receptionist, Mikhail stepped behind her and stuck a hypodermic into her neck, pushing its plunger.

"Hey! What do you—"

The fast-acting poison made the woman shudder. Five seconds later, she slumped across her desk.

The other men took off their outdoor gloves, revealing latex ones. In a carefully rehearsed sequence, Mikhail grabbed the receptionist's pass key off the desk, returned to the start of the corridor, and used the key to open a door to a custodial area. Kagan and Yakov picked up the dead woman and carried her through the open door, setting the corpse inside. When they returned to the corridor, they pulled the door shut, automatically locking it.

Meanwhile, Andrei and Viktor went up a curved staircase and faced the three doors that led to the target's suite.

The others joined them.

Andrei looked at his watch and nodded. Everything was proceeding as planned. Six minutes earlier, at 8:00 P.M., they'd stood amid the snowfall on the tourist-crowded Plaza, watching Hassan, his wife, and four protective escorts get into a limousine bound for a reception at the New Mexico governor's mansion. At 9:00, Hassan was scheduled to step before television cameras and deliver the first of many rousing speeches about his newborn child of peace and his hopes for the Middle East.

But just before the speech, Hassan's wife would receive a call on her cell phone. She would answer because the number displayed on the phone belonged to her baby's nursemaid.

The voice would belong to a man, however. It would explain in vivid detail what had happened to the baby. It would emphasize that if Hassan loved his child, he would cancel the speech.

And never make another one.

KAGAN STARED through the window, straining to distinguish shadows from illusions in the falling snow.

One of them will try to distract me in the front, he thought. *Probably Andrei. I set up enough ambushes with him. That's how he thinks. Meanwhile, Mikhail and Yakov will attack from the sides.*

But wouldn't they have made their move by now? Kagan wondered. *Maybe I did fool them. It's been a while. Maybe nothing's going to happen. Maybe they're back on Canyon Road.*

The baby whimpered.

"Meredith," Kagan said.

"He's just restless. Probably having another dream."

"Doesn't sound like a happy one."

"I put my little finger to his lips. He's sucking on it. He's quiet now."

"You can't let him cry."

"He's a good baby. He won't cry."

Kagan never looked in Meredith's direction. With the gun on his lap, he focused intently on the window.

He continued with the story, working to keep Cole and Meredith calm, hoping it would overcome his fatigue and keep him alert.

"In those days, the capital of Israel was Jerusalem. The man in charge was a Roman puppet named Herod, who called himself the king of the Jews. He was seriously paranoid. Forty years earlier, a rebellion had chased him from Israel. The Romans had hit back viciously, using thousands of battle-hardened soldiers to return Herod to power. Thereafter, he squashed the slightest sign of a rebellion, even to the point of killing one of his wives, her mother, and several of his sons.

"Now, suddenly at dawn, the guards on the eastern wall of Jerusalem reported three strangers coming out of the distance, approaching on camels. Their confident bearing identified them as men of importance. When they reached the gate, they announced that they were priests on a sacred mission and asked to pay their respects to Herod. What do you suppose his reaction was, Cole?"

"He wouldn't have liked them surprising him like that."

"You bet, especially when the Magi came from Israel's biggest, closest enemy. He was furious and demanded an explanation from his security team. How had the Magi traveled all the way to Jerusalem without being detected? Why had the Roman soldiers failed to intercept them? What sort of protection did he have if foreigners could pass through the desert as though they were invisible?

"I told you that the Magi had a reputation for being a secret group with magical powers. Now, when they were brought before Herod, they described an amazing star that had led them to Jerusalem. Herod was astonished. 'A star?' he asked. 'What kind of star?'

"The Magi answered, 'A star that announces the birth of the new king of the Jews.'"

Kagan heard footsteps—Meredith bringing the coffee. He started to tell her to keep low, but he didn't need to. She made him proud by crouching beside him, staying beneath the level of the window.

"Thanks." Keeping his right hand on the gun in his lap, he ignored the pain of using his stiff left arm to raise the cup to his lips. He blew on the steaming liquid, then sipped, inhaling its fragrance, tasting the sugar.

"The water you put on the stove is boiling," Meredith said.

"Good. Keep it boiling. Add more water if it gets low." Kagan never removed his gaze from the window. He listened to Meredith as she crawled across the floor and sat next to the baby.

"Where was I, Cole?" Kagan didn't need reminding, but he wanted to keep the boy answering questions.

"Herod and the star."

"Right." Again, the spymaster's words came back to him from years earlier. "All through the Jewish and Roman world at that time, there was a growing belief that ancient prophecies were about to be fulfilled, that someone special would soon be born and the course of history would change. In the Old Testament Book of Daniel, which is set hundreds of years earlier, Daniel had a vision about a sign in the heavens bringing a mysterious leader who would establish a new, everlasting dominion.

"There were many similar predictions. Even contemporary Roman historians like Suetonius and Tacitus mentioned prophecies about a man from Israel who would rule the world. One of the great Roman poets, Virgil, predicted that a child would descend from the heavens, possibly from the constellation Virgo, or Virgin, and establish a golden age."

"Sounds like he was talking about the Virgin Mary," Cole said, puzzled.

"Or maybe there's another explanation. Maybe Virgil was trying to impress someone of influence, a politician perhaps, whose wife was about to give birth and whom Virgil was praising for her virtue. Presumably the child would be the divine creator of peace that Virgil predicted in his poem. He might even have been referring to the Roman emperor.

"There can be all sorts of explanations for those prophecies. But that's not the point. What matters is that two thousand years ago, people believed them—really believed them.

"Herod certainly did. When he heard about the magical star, he went berserk and summoned his priests, demanding to know what they thought of the Magi's claims. 'A star indeed exists in many of the prophecies,' the priests agreed. Herod shouted, 'But do the prophecies say where the new king will be born?' The priests answered, 'Yes.' They quoted an ancient text that said, 'And you, Bethlehem, are by no means insignificant since from you shall come a leader of Israel.'

"'Bethlehem,' Herod murmured. Now remember, Cole, this was a power-hungry sociopath who killed his own sons because he suspected they were plotting against him. What would he do if he believed a new rival threatened his throne? He was in his seventies, and terrified of losing control. Even though he'd probably be dead by the time the child was old enough to threaten him, the child's followers were another matter. If a revolution was being planned, Herod needed to stop it with every means possible. Cole, what do you suppose was actually going on?"

"I don't understand."

"The Magi were spies. What do you think their mission was? They arrived as if by magic and told a story about an amazing star and a newborn rival. What was the point of telling him?"

"It sure made him angry."

"And? Draw a conclusion."

"Maybe that was the point—to make him angry."

"You definitely have the instincts of a spy. Using prophecies, along with their reputation for secret knowledge that supposedly enabled them to predict the future, the Magi set forces in motion to destabilize Herod and his government."

"Destabilize?"

"Make it fall apart. From an espionage point of view, the tactic was brilliant. If Herod ordered all his men to root out every sign of an imagined rebellion, if the mysterious child was reported everywhere throughout the kingdom, Herod wouldn't be able to focus on ruling the country. Persia could intensify its attacks on Israel's border while Herod's defenses became so chaotic that the country collapsed from within. The Roman Empire wouldn't know how to retaliate because the fall of Israel would have been caused by Herod himself."

"It's like you said." Cole sounded impressed. "What they did was more powerful than fighting a battle."

"If the plan had worked. But Herod showed how clever he was and why he'd been able to stay in power for so many years. His instincts warned him about the potential for a trap. Not that he suspected the Magi. Even his own priests admitted that the newcomers had the authority of the prophets.

"No, it was Bethlehem that bothered him. Only eight miles south of Jerusalem, the town lay in a rich agricultural area, where the inhabitants had ample money to organize a revolution. It was nestled among hills that would be easy to defend and difficult to attack. Its proximity to Jerusalem made it all the more suspect, since raids on the capital would be easy to stage from there.

"In his rage, Herod almost ordered his army to ransack Bethlehem until they found the child and killed him. But he feared he might cause the rebellion he wanted to suppress. So he decided to try a different approach, and the idea he came up with was so unexpected that even the Magi were caught unprepared.

"He tried to recruit them as his own unwitting spies. 'The child you came looking for has a magnificent destiny,' he told them. 'Continue your journey. Go to Bethlehem. Find the savior that the star predicted. Worship him. Then come back here and tell me where the child is so that I, too, might go and worship him.'

"How classic. The Magi were so convincing that Herod didn't realize who his true enemies were. They became what intelligence experts call double agents: spies pretending to work for one side when they're actually working for the other.

"They must have been terribly pleased as they traveled south to Bethlehem. Now that they had Herod's trust, they could tell him anything they wanted to, and he'd believe them. More than they'd originally hoped, their made-up reports would cause Herod to order his soldiers back and forth across the kingdom, fatally weakening his defenses as he chased a phantom. But something remarkable happened in Bethlehem, something that changed everything."

"What was *that*?" Cole asked.

"They began to believe that the disinformation they'd given Herod was in fact the truth."

"You understand what you're supposed to do?" Andrei asked Brody. "Learn as much as you can. Talk about it as naturally as possible so the suspect doesn't realize we're listening. We're particularly interested in any defenses he set up."

"Yes," Brody said, "but . . . "

"Are you having second thoughts? You don't want to help your wife and son? You don't want to make up for beating her?"

"Honest to God, I've never regretted anything more in my life."

"Then prove it to them. Maybe you can convince the suspect that we're not out here, that he's safe and he can let your family go."

"But . . ."

Andrei cut him off. "Okay, if you don't want to help your wife and son, fine. I can understand why you don't want to risk your own neck. It's human nature to look out for number one. When the SWAT team gets their snipers set up, I'll figure another way to handle this."

"Snipers? For heaven's sake, *no*."

"Mr. Brody, I don't have a lot of alternatives."

"All right, all right. I'll go in there."

"You're sure? No second thoughts?"

"I said I'll do it!"

"Keep your voice down. The suspect might hear you."

"Sorry. This is all too—"

Andrei put a steadying hand on Brody's shoulder. "Your family'll be proud of you. That's what matters. Now there are just a couple of other details. Give me your keys."

"My keys? Why?"

"Is there a vehicle in your garage?"

"A Range Rover."

"The suspect might try to escape in it. Canyon Road should be open to traffic by now. He might be tempted to take the chance."

Brody gave Andrei the keys. "But if Canyon Road's open to traffic now, why hasn't the SWAT team gotten here? It's been a long time."

"Good question. I'll call headquarters and find out." Andrei pulled out Brody's cell phone, opened it, started to press numbers, and again deliberately lost his grip. As he intended, it fell in the snow.

"Damn," Andrei said. "I wish I'd worn thick gloves. My hands are so cold I can barely hold anything."

He reached into the snow, groped, and pulled out the phone. He brushed snow from it and pretended to try to use it.

"Shit. Now *this* phone's not working, either." He didn't want Brody going into the house with a phone. Pyotyr would no doubt find it and use it to get help. "I'm awfully sorry about this. You'd better lend me your wife's phone."

"Lend you . . . ?" Brody tensed. "What's going on here?"

"Don't worry. The police department will get you a new one," Andrei promised.

"What did you say your name was?"

"I didn't. It's Detective Parker."

"You told me your microphones and earbuds allow you to communicate with headquarters, so why do you need my wife's phone? This is . . . Something's wrong. Let me see your badge."

"Badge?"

"All of you. Let me see your ID."

"I told you to keep your voice down," Andrei warned. "My identification's under my coat." He brushed snow from the front. "Do you really want me to freeze, just so you can—"

Brody backed away.

"What are you doing, Mr. Brody?"

As Brody turned to run down the shadowy lane, Andrei shoved him hard, knocking him into the snow. He bent down, braced a heavy knee on Brody's back, and rammed his face down into a drift. Andrei's powerful hand kept Brody's features submerged in the snow.

Brody struggled, gagging, but Andrei ignored his efforts and pressed his face down harder into the drift.

"Listen to me," Andrei whispered close to Brody's left ear. "You're going to do what I want, or I'll smother you. Do you feel the snow clogging your nostrils? Some of it's melting. You're inhaling the water. Soon you'll be choking."

Pinned in the drift, Brody started coughing. The sound was muffled by the snow. His back arched—or tried to. His chest heaved.

"Are you listening?" Andrei asked quietly, applying more weight to his back. "Do you want to die in a snowbank on Christmas Eve, or would you like to spend the holiday with your wife and son?"

Brody choked as he tried to speak under the snow.

At once, Andrei reached under Brody's hat, grabbed his hair, and jerked his head up. Brody's cheeks were covered with snow. He strained to clear his nose and mouth, but Andrei pressed a glove over his face to diminish the sound.

"What are the names of your wife and son?" Andrei murmured. He took his hand from Brody's mouth while he pressed his Glock to Brody's right temple.

Snot clung to Brody's mustache.

"Meredith. My wife's name is Meredith. My son . . . my son is Cole."

"Nice names. I bet they're wonderful people. *Are* they?"

"Yes."

"Do you love them, Ted?" The tip of the sound suppressor on Andrei's Glock made an indentation in Brody's skin. Andrei imagined how hard and cold the metal felt.

"Love them?" Brody managed to answer. "Of course."

"Prove it, Ted. Prove that you love Meredith and Cole. Prove how much you wish you hadn't punched your wife. This is your chance to be a hero. Save them. Save your family, Ted."

"Yes." Brody trembled. "I'll do anything for them."

"Then nothing's different. You'll go in that house. You'll notice whatever defenses have been set up. You'll ask about them. We'll hear you talking. We'll know what to expect."

"Meredith and Cole . . . "

"We take care of people who cooperate, Ted. I just thought of something." Andrei felt a sudden terrible doubt. "Is there a computer in your house? Could the man in there have e-mailed for help?"

"I use a password lock."

Andrei breathed out, releasing some of his tension.

"Good," he said. "Before we go into the house, I'll tell you we're coming. You'll have plenty of warning. All you need to do is get your family down to the floor. As soon as we teach a lesson to our friend in there, and retrieve something he stole from us, we'll leave. You and your wife and son can have a nice life."

"God, don't I wish."

"What he stole from us is crucial. I want you to make sure we get it back alive."

"Alive?"

"It's a baby."

"A . . . What's a *baby* doing in there?"

"That's not your concern, Ted. Just talk about the baby when you see it. Tell me where it is. When we go inside, I want to make sure it isn't injured."

"But what about my family?"

"I told you, just get them onto the floor. I promise, you and your wife and your son will be safe. An hour from now, this'll be over. We'll be gone. Your family will owe their lives to you. You'll be a hero to them. Your wife won't have any choice except to forgive you for hitting her. Do you understand, Ted? Is everything clear?"

KAGAN STOOD *with Andrei, Mikhail, Yakov, and the new man, Viktor, in the corridor outside the three doors. Beyond the middle door, he heard the muffled sound of a television, the only noise in the corridor. All the other guests were probably away from their rooms, enjoying the holiday festivities.*

As adrenaline surged through him, Kagan heard just enough of the television program to be able to determine that a little girl was asking someone if he was really Santa Claus. The voice of an elderly man said that he was.

That middle room was where the three bodyguards were based.

Concentrating to control his breathing, Kagan watched Andrei take his cell phone from his pocket. It was set to the vibrate mode, and what Andrei waited for was a call from the nursemaid in the suite. Not that Andrei would answer the call. All he needed was to feel the vibration through his glove.

He also needed to verify the caller's number. It would signal that the nursemaid had rigged the door to the left, pressing a strip of plastic against the spring-controlled latch, preventing it from sliding into the door frame and locking the door. She had done the same with the door on the right.

By now, she would have taken the baby into the bathroom, where the two of them would be lying in the bathtub.

The bathtub wasn't sturdy enough to keep bullets from penetrating it, but shots weren't likely to go in that direction. As a precaution, however, Hassan's rivals had bribed the nursemaid to lie sideways, with her back to the closed bathroom door, holding the baby on the other side so that if a chance bullet did come into the bathroom, the baby would have a human shield.

Andrei's phone made a faint buzzing sound. He looked at the screen to view the caller's number. He nodded to the team, put the phone away, and drew the Glock from his coat pocket.

Kagan and the others pulled out their weapons. A sound suppressor projected from each barrel.

Each man eased back the slide on his pistol just enough to assure that a round was in the firing chamber. They'd performed this precaution several times prior to starting the mission, but no matter how often they'd already done so, they felt compelled to do it yet again, an obsessive habit of gunfighters.

Kagan's hands were sweaty in his latex gloves.

Andrei nodded a final time. The team separated, Kagan and Mikhail going to the door on the right, beyond which, they'd been told, the nursemaid rested when Hassan's wife took care of the baby. Yakov and Viktor proceeded to the door on the far left, while Andrei—who liked frontal distractions—went to the middle door.

Andrei knocked loudly on the middle door, no doubt startling the bodyguards beyond it. Kagan pressed a hand against the door on the right at the exact moment Yakov did the same to the door on the far left.

For an urgent second, Kagan met resistance and wondered if the nursemaid's strip of plastic had in fact kept the latch from engaging, but then Andrei knocked louder on the middle door, and when Kagan pushed, his door came open. Mikhail immediately aimed past him, making sure the room was unoccupied.

Andrei pounded on the middle door a third time, saying, "Housekeeping!" in a loud voice while Kagan and Mikhail hurried into the room on the right. As the nursemaid had promised, the connecting door was open. Kagan pretended that the bed was in his way, allowing Mikhail to charge ahead and crouch, firing upward toward chest and head level in the middle room.

Mikhail's sound suppressor made the shots barely audible. Amid the smell of burned gunpowder, Kagan hurried next to him and fired upward, his bullets striking bodyguards who were in effect already dead. In the opposite open doorway, Yakov and Viktor crouched and also fired upward, the angle of their aim preventing them from being caught in a crossfire.

Blood spurted from the three bodyguards. Groaning, they fell in a cluster, one of them landing on the other two.

Mikhail stepped into the room and shot each man in the head.

Kagan ran back through the bedroom toward the door he'd shoved open. He leaned into the corridor and motioned for Andrei to enter. The moment Andrei hurried past him, Kagan tore off the plastic strip attached to the side of the door, allowing the latch to function again. He shut the door and turned the dead bolt, then followed Andrei into the middle room, where the coppery smell of blood was now strong.

They stepped over the bodies and joined the rest of the team in the third bedroom, the outer door to which Yakov had closed and locked.

Andrei knocked three times on the bathroom door, twice, then once, completing the all-clear signal.

After a pause, the door was unlocked. As it came open, Kagan saw a Palestinian woman. Her veil made it difficult to tell how old she was or what she looked like, but she had dark, expressive eyes that communicated her nervousness. She wore a black head scarf and a modest, loose black dress.

She held an Arab baby in her arms. The child wore a blue sleeper and was wrapped in a blanket.

Frightened, the woman looked past Andrei and his men toward the middle room.

"It's finished," Andrei said.

She knew enough English to understand.

Andrei held out a thick envelope. "Here's the remainder of what you're owed. Give us the baby."

The woman frowned at the envelope, as if wishing that she'd never agreed to be part of this.

"Take the money," Andrei said. "You earned it. Go far away."

The woman hesitated.

"Viktor," Andrei said, "get the baby from her."

Viktor did what he was told. The infant sensed the less comforting grip and squirmed.

The woman looked troubled.

"Don't worry. He'll be fine," Andrei assured her.

As she took the envelope, Yakov shot her twice in the chest and once in the head. She toppled back, landing on the white tiles of the bathroom floor. Yakov stepped over her blood and yanked the envelope from her hand.

"THE NEXT PART of the story isn't in Matthew's gospel," Kagan said. "It's in Luke's, where we're told that the Roman emperor issued a census decree."

He swallowed coffee. Needing the energy it provided, he felt his dry mouth absorb the hot liquid. His right hand remained on the pistol in his lap.

"The census was important for a lot of reasons. It established a population base on which Rome could demand taxes from Israel. But it also forced the Jews to travel, sometimes far, and thus reminded them that they were at the emperor's beck and call."

"Why were they forced to travel?" Cole asked.

"Because each family had to register according to the tribe—what they called the house—that the husband belonged to. To do that, they needed to go to whatever town was originally associated with that tribe. This is where Mary and Joseph get involved. They lived to the north in Nazareth, but Joseph belonged to the house of David, and the town associated with David was Bethlehem, seventy-five miles to the south. It was a difficult journey over several deep canyons. To complicate matters, Mary was far along in her pregnancy, which meant that they needed to be careful, taking even longer than usual to get there. As a consequence, when they finally reached Bethlehem, a lot of people had arrived sooner, and there weren't any places for them to stay. No room at the inn, as Luke's gospel says."

In the darkness, Kagan finished the coffee and leaned down, ignoring the pain in his wounded arm as he set the cup on the floor. But he never took his eyes from the window. Now the snow fell so thickly that the fence was a blur.

"Mary and Joseph were reduced to sleeping in a stable. Mary gave birth there, and the only spot to put the baby was a manger. That's a trough from which animals eat. If you ever go to Bethlehem, Cole, you'll find a cave that's advertised as the place where Jesus was born. Maybe it's true. Bethlehem has a lot of limestone slopes, and in those days, people carved stables into the limestone. I like the idea of a cave. It's more defensible than a mere stable.

"The crèche next to your Christmas tree has the Magi in the stable, greeting Mary, Joseph, and the newborn Jesus. But that wasn't the case. Matthew says the Magi entered a house, where they found Jesus and his mother. Similar details suggest that the Magi arrived some time after Jesus was born.

"The moment they got to Bethlehem, they did what Herod expected, asking about newborn children and whether there were any unusual circumstances about the birth. If you want my opinion, the last thing they anticipated was to find evidence supporting their story. Their purpose was to give disinformation to Herod and back it up by any means possible. So when they heard about a birth in a stable, they probably decided it was the kind of detail they could use—a great king born in humble conditions. The contrast with Herod's greed would drive him crazy.

"But as the Magi checked further, trying to manufacture an elaborate hoax to continue fooling Herod, they heard about something else that was unusual about the birth, and *that* changed everything for them."

"What was it?" Cole asked.

"Something that involved the other group in the crèche next to your Christmas tree. You already mentioned them."

"The shepherds?"

"Yes. Word had spread through Bethlehem about something weird that had happened to the shepherds. The night the baby was born, they were out in a dark field, tending their sheep, when a mysterious figure suddenly appeared, surrounded by a blazing light. The figure told them to rejoice, to go into Bethlehem and look for a newborn baby in a stable, for this baby was special, a savior. Abruptly, other brilliant figures appeared to the shepherds, announcing, 'Glory to God in the highest. Peace on Earth.' Then they all vanished, leaving the shepherds alone in the dark.

"Frankly, Cole, if that had happened to me, I think I might have had a heart attack. But the shepherds were made of stronger stuff. They adjusted to their shock and were so curious that they decided to go into Bethlehem to see if what the mysterious figure had told them was true. Just as predicted, they found the baby in the stable.

"That's what the Magi heard the villagers talking about. Immediately, they asked where they could find the shepherds and were given directions to the field where the vision had supposedly happened. There they got the story firsthand. It was exactly the sort of event that would have held their attention. Remember, the Magi believed in magic. Intrigued, they asked where the stable was, where they could find the baby, but as Matthew's gospel indicates, by then Mary and Jesus were in a house.

"It's interesting that the gospel doesn't mention Joseph at this point. I have a theory about him, but I'll save it until later. For now, the important thing is that the Magi were experts in elicitation."

"I don't know what that is," Cole said.

"It's the art of making people trust you so much that they volunteer information they normally wouldn't feel comfortable revealing. By subtly imitating speech patterns and body movements, even the way people breathe, you can make strangers feel as if they've known you for a very long time. The Magi were so skilled at it that they persuaded Mary to tell them some very personal details. Among other things, she described how visions had come to her, similar to the apparitions the shepherds had seen in the field. She explained that when she and Joseph were engaged to be married . . . Meredith, how frankly can I talk about the pregnancy?"

Cole answered for her. "If you mean sex and virginity and stuff like that, I guess I know enough that you don't need to be embarrassed."

"Me?" Kagan asked. "Embarrassed?"

"It's okay," Meredith said. "I have a feeling he'll know what you're talking about."

She almost sounded amused.

Good, Kagan thought. *They're distracted.*

He stared out the window and managed to find the words to continue.

"Joseph was engaged to Mary, but before they became husband and wife, Mary told him she was pregnant. Because Joseph knew he wasn't the father, he naturally assumed she'd been with another man, but Mary swore that she'd been faithful. She said that an angel had come to her and announced that even though she was a virgin, she'd conceived through the Holy Spirit.

"So what was Joseph to do? He could accuse Mary of infidelity and cast her aside, or else he could take her word that an angel had spoken to her about a miraculous conception.

"It was a difficult, painful choice. Joseph felt betrayed. But at the same time, he loved Mary with all his heart. Distraught, he considered one option and then the other, weighing them, unable to decide. Anger versus love.

"Emotionally exhausted, he fell asleep, and all of a sudden, he had a dream in which a brilliant figure—an angel—appeared before him. The angel told him the exact same thing that Mary had insisted an angel had told *her:* that the Holy Spirit was the father.

"The dream is significant because the house of David to which Joseph belonged had a tradition of believing in the truth of dreams, and of being able to interpret them. But surely Joseph must have wondered if his tortured thoughts had caused the dream, or if an angel really had come to him. It all amounted to this—was he willing to reject the woman he loved because she was pregnant with a child that wasn't his? In the end, he chose to believe in his dream. He swallowed his pride and proved his love by marrying her."

The baby whimpered.

"Meredith?"

"His diaper's still dry. Maybe he's thirsty again. I'll bring more of that mixture."

As the baby's voice rose, Kagan heard Meredith hurry into the kitchen. He heard the scrape of the saucepan as she poured what was left of the mixture into the shot glass. She rushed back and sat on the floor, lifting the baby into her arms.

A moment later, the baby was quiet.

"He's drinking, but he's awfully restless," Meredith said.

Are you sending me a message? Kagan wondered. *Is this the same thing that happened when you kicked me, and I thought you were guiding me here?*

He shook his head. *Get real*, he thought. *I'm still off balance from being wounded.*

"So Joseph married her," Kagan said. His temples felt the pressure of his urgent heartbeat. "There was a problem, though. Mary's pregnancy would soon start to show. *Too* soon. Like nosy people everywhere, the good folks in Nazareth would start asking questions, and you can bet *they* wouldn't believe what Mary said about the angel. The scandal would make her an outcast.

"That's when Mary learned that one of her relatives, Elizabeth, also was pregnant. Elizabeth lived a distance away in a town called Judah, and Mary decided to go there—'in haste,' Luke's gospel says. She stayed three months, helping with the household until Elizabeth's baby was born, but then it was time for Mary to return to Nazareth, where the townspeople would certainly have noticed that she was more pregnant than she should be. When Mary and Joseph heard about the Roman census decree, they realized they had a perfect excuse to leave town. Required by law to go to Bethlehem and register, they wouldn't have taken long to pack.

"Over a period of time, the Magi elicited this account from Mary. It was an amazing match to what the shepherds had told them about being visited by angels. The parallels were astonishing, and these priests who believed in dreams and magic wouldn't have dismissed them. On the contrary, the Magi would have investigated in greater detail, questioning the people in Bethlehem, looking for inconsistencies and contradictions, anything to cast doubt on what was being said.

But after all their efforts, the Magi concluded that the stories were genuine, that the disinformation they'd fed Herod in an effort to destabilize his government was, in ways too mysterious to understand, the truth.

"I was with a group of spies when I first heard this interpretation of the Christmas story," Kagan said. For a moment, he felt nostalgic. He'd been eighteen the first time he'd heard it. *Fourteen years ago*, Kagan thought.

And now I'm an old man.

"One of those spies said he could make a case that the Magi themselves were victims of disinformation."

"What do you mean?" Cole asked.

"Their sudden appearance in Jerusalem would have been widely reported. Herod's furious reaction to what they said about the star and the newborn king would have been widely reported as well. Herod was an unpopular ruler. His fears about a rebellion were justified. Perhaps a rebel spy in Herod's court learned that the king was sending the Magi to Bethlehem to search for the child. The rebels could have arranged for the shepherds and Mary to tell the Magi a story that elaborated on what the Magi had told Herod. Perhaps the Magi were deceived, just as they had deceived Herod."

"Deceived?" Meredith asked.

"The rebels couldn't have known that the Magi were foreign spies. They couldn't have known that the Magi wanted to destabilize Herod's government. So they told the Magi stories that they hoped the Magi would take back to Herod, further unbalancing the king. Perhaps the shepherds and

Mary were rebels. Perhaps they wanted the same thing the Magi did, but neither side realized they were working toward a common goal."

"Makes my head spin," Meredith said.

"That's what the spy world is like. A U.S. spymaster—who might actually have worked for the Soviets—once called espionage a wilderness of mirrors."

"But I don't want to believe that Mary and the shepherds were pretending."

"Neither do I," Kagan replied. "And as far as I'm concerned, the rest of the story proves they weren't."

The baby made a sound.

Kagan tensed.

"He's more restless," Meredith said.

Kagan's apprehension strengthened. "I'd better finish."

"YOU'RE SURE the same house key fits all the doors?" Andrei asked.

"Yes," Brody answered.

"Good. Then this doesn't need to be difficult. Go into the house. Act surprised when you see the intruder. Ask the natural questions about whatever traps you notice he's arranged. Find out where the baby is."

"But the guy'll see that I'm nervous," Brody said. "He might suspect that I'm working for you."

"Of *course* he'll see that you're nervous. That's the beauty of the situation. You beat up your wife. You're terrified that she'll leave you. You come to beg her to forgive you. Then you discover there's a stranger in the house. Who wouldn't be nervous? He'll never guess what's really going on. Just do what we rehearsed. Tomorrow morning, you and your family can open your Christmas presents. Tonight will be just a bad memory."

"I hope to God you're right."

Andrei gave Brody's arm an encouraging squeeze.

"You'll do this perfectly. I have faith in you."

He watched Brody walk uneasily through the falling snow toward the gate.

The moment Brody was too far away to hear what he said, Andrei turned to his companions.

"Yakov, as soon as Brody's inside, go to the left side of the house. Mikhail, go to the right. Use one of the metal chairs Brody told us about, and position it under a window in the master bedroom. Because you gave Brody your earbud and microphone, you and I will stay in contact via our cell phones while Yakov monitors the radio conversation. After we learn where the baby is and where the booby traps are, I'll say, 'Merry Christmas' to Brody. That's my signal to both of you. A second later, I'll shoot out the front window and attack through there.

"At the same time, Mikhail, you'll stand on the metal chair and go through a window in the back bedroom. The noise will keep Pyotyr from hearing Yakov turn the key in the side door and charge in. We'll be shooting from three different directions. There'll be so much disruption, Pyotyr won't know where to turn first. Plus, all those people will be in the way, screaming, panicking, interfering with his aim.

"When I picked up the cell phone Pyotyr lost, I also found his spare magazines. They must have been in the same coat pocket. Without enough ammunition to fight all of us, what chance does he have?"

"You don't want Brody and his family injured?" Mikhail asked.

"On the contrary. They can't be allowed to tell the police anything. I want them all dead. Except the baby. We can't attack until we know where the baby is."

THE COPPERY ODOR *of the nursemaid's blood filled Kagan's nostrils. He watched Yakov draw his thumb across the cash in the thick envelope he'd taken from the woman's corpse.*

Andrei held out his hand.

"What?" Yakov asked.

"Our clients might want the bribe money returned to them," Andrei said. "Give it to me."

"And if they don't remember to ask for the money?"

"Then the Pakhan will want his cut."

Surprising Kagan, it was Viktor who spoke next, not Yakov. "Always the Pakhan," the gangly newcomer said, holding the baby.

Andrei ignored him. "Yakov, I want the envelope."

With a sigh, Yakov gave it to him.

"After the Pakhan takes his cut, I'll divide the money evenly," *Andrei promised.*

"We'll make sure you do." Viktor tightened his grip on the squirming baby.

Andrei turned toward him. "You're new, Viktor. You're still learning how things work here, so I'll make an exception just this once. But never challenge me again."

Viktor's eyes became fierce. "Yakov challenged you also. Give him *shit, the same as you do me."*

"Yakov challenged me? I don't think so."

Viktor glowered. "Whatever you say."

"Now you're getting the idea. Whatever I say."

The baby whimpered in Viktor's arms. The sound—and the helplessness it conveyed—stirred something in Kagan.

"Give the package to Mikhail," Andrei said.

"But I can handle it," Viktor objected.

"It doesn't like you. Do as we rehearsed and give the baby to Mikhail before you make it cry."

Kagan watched Andrei step close to the baby and concentrate on its small, unhappy face. An odd emotion seemed to cross Andrei's own face, a feeling he apparently found so unusual that it baffled him. As Viktor gave the struggling baby to Mikhail, Andrei shook his head, giving the impression that he forcibly subdued the unfamiliar emotion. He stuffed the envelope into an inside pocket of his ski jacket, then pressed the microphone that was hidden under the ski-lift tickets on the jacket.

"This is Melchior. We have the package. We're leaving the store. Two minutes."

Viktor and Yakov opened the bedroom door and checked to make certain the hallway was deserted before stepping out of the room. They put their weapons in their coats and motioned for Mikhail to follow with the baby. Kagan and Andrei went last, concealing their pistols, making sure the door was locked behind them.

As they'd rehearsed, Kagan hung a DO NOT DISTURB *sign on the doorknob. The television continued to murmur in the suite, the elderly man's voice still maintaining that he was Santa Claus.*

They went down the curved staircase and walked along the carpeted hallway, passing the desk where the receptionist had greeted them before Mikhail had killed her.

Viktor opened the security door that isolated this exclusive group of rooms from the rest of the hotel. Keeping Mikhail and the baby in the middle, the group passed the elevator, opened a fire door, and went down a harshly lit concrete stairwell. As they descended, they took off their latex gloves and put on their outdoor ones.

The baby's whimper echoed amid their scraping footsteps.

"This is Melchior. One minute till arrival," Andrei said to his microphone.

Three floors down, they reached the street level. Here a security camera was aimed at the corridor. They kept their heads down and tightened their two-one-two formation, partially shielding Mikhail in the middle so the camera couldn't see the baby in his arms.

Through a glass door—the side exit from the hotel—Kagan saw snow falling past murky streetlights. Warmly dressed people walked past the window. Beyond vehicles parked along the curb, a dark van suddenly stopped.

I can't do this, *Kagan thought.*

That afternoon, for a long time, he'd knelt in the nearby cathedral and stared at a manger scene, trying to tell himself that his controllers were absolutely right, that the innocent lives he'd saved were all that mattered. "Bring me home," he'd begged them in dead-drop messages during the past three months. Sometimes he'd managed to slip away from Andrei and risk phone calls. But there had always been some reason his controllers couldn't bring him in. He was too well placed, they'd insisted. No one could ever hope to penetrate the Russian mob so deeply. If he disappeared, the Russians would realize he was a spy, making it more dangerous to try to infiltrate another operative into the heart of their organization.

"Then fake my death," Kagan had urged them. "The Russians won't suspect I was a mole if they think I'm dead." But his controllers had talked of new rumors, about plastic explosives, handheld missiles, and biological weapons being smuggled in via ports controlled by the Odessa Mafia. They'd reminded him of all the innocent lives he had an obligation to save.

Meanwhile, he'd obeyed the Pakhan's orders to burn homes, break arms and legs, yank out teeth, and beat up women. More of his soul had disintegrated.

Viktor and Yakov stepped from the hotel and looked both ways, staring at pedestrians in the shadowy snowfall. With a nod, they signaled to Mikhail to carry the baby outside. Andrei and Kagan followed.

Kagan's cheeks felt cold. His stomach felt colder.

Too much, *he thought.* No more.

The group passed between snow-covered cars parked along the curb. Headlights glowed in the street. Reaching the van, Viktor pulled its side door open. Yakov scrambled in. Mikhail approached with the baby. Andrei and Kagan followed.

The baby squirmed in Mikhail's arms.

I wanted to make the world better, *Kagan thought.*

The baby cried. Mikhail held it with one arm while using his free hand to grip an armrest in the van and climb in.

"Don't drop it," *Andrei warned.*

I wanted to fight the kind of men who made my parents afraid for so many years, *Kagan thought.*

The baby struggled as Mikhail sat next to Yakov opposite the side door.

And now I'm no different from the people I set out to fight.

Kagan let Andrei climb in next. With the middle seat occupied, Andrei was forced to squeeze toward the seat in the back.

I've beaten. I've tortured. I've killed, *Kagan thought.* But by God, this is one thing I won't do.

He leaned into the van, as if to reach for an armrest and climb all the way in. His heart pounding, he pointed in feigned alarm.

"What happened to the baby? It's bleeding!"

"What?" *Mikhail asked.* "Where?" *He opened his arms to examine the child.*

Kagan grabbed it, surged back from the open door, felt Viktor behind him, and swung. Something tugged violently at his coat, but only for a moment. With both arms gripping the baby, Kagan focused on his right elbow. He pivoted with such force that when the tip of the elbow struck Viktor's nose, he felt the bones crack. They shattered and propelled inward with such power that Kagan knew they'd pierced Viktor's brain.

Hearing shouts of alarm coming from the open van, he charged up the street, veered between cars at the curb, reached the sidewalk, and shouted for pedestrians to get out of his way. All at once, his left arm jerked, then became numb.

He'd been hit by a bullet. The sound suppressor on the gun that had fired it prevented bystanders from knowing why glass had shattered in front of him.

That's the last shot they'll fire, *he desperately hoped.* Andrei won't take the chance of a stray bullet hitting the baby.

As he hurried through the crowd, Kagan used his now-awkward left arm to pull down the zipper on his parka. The numbness changed to searing pain. Imagining Andrei, Yakov, and Mikhail scrambling from the van, he shoved the baby under his coat and pulled up the zipper to provide warmth.

Andrei would immediately chase him, Kagan knew. Yakov and perhaps Mikhail would drag Viktor's body into the van before the pedestrians could realize what had happened and start a panic. Then the two killers would join the hunt.

Andrei's voice shouted through his earbud.

"Pyotyr, what the hell are you doing?"

Kagan increased his speed, shouldering past people on the sidewalk.

"Pyotyr, bring back the package!"

Instead of answering, Kagan took deep breaths and rushed toward the cathedral that towered at the end of the narrow street. The baby nestled against him, warm and surprisingly calm against his stomach.

I'll protect you, *he silently promised.* I'll do everything in my power to keep you safe.

He looked for a police car, tempted to ask for help, but immediately he realized that during the time it would take to explain, Andrei and the others would catch up. They would shoot Kagan and the policeman in the head and take the baby.

Phone for backup, *he told himself. Desperate to contact his controllers, he used his stiffening arm to reach for the cell phone in the left pocket of his coat. He felt dizzy when he discovered that the pocket was torn open, that his cell phone was missing, along with his spare ammunition. He remembered something tugging at the side of his coat. Someone must have lunged to try to stop him and snagged that pocket.*

Have a plan, a backup plan, and then a backup plan after that. *Kagan's instructors had hammered that into him.* Visualize what you're going to do. Rehearse it in your mind, even if you can't rehearse it physically. Never do anything without knowing your options.

But Kagan's decision to take the baby had been made on the spot. Even though he'd agonized about it that afternoon in front of the cathedral's manger, he hadn't made up his mind until the moment he'd leaned into the van and told Mikhail, "The baby's bleeding!"

Where am I going? *Kagan thought in desperation.*

Ahead, he saw a crowd on the street to the right of the cathedral. Hundreds of people walked with purpose. Under his parka, the baby kicked him, as if urging him to follow.

"Pyotyr!" *Andrei's angry voice pierced through Kagan's earbud.* "I found your cell phone! You're on your own! You can't get help! Bring back the package!"

Breathing hard, wincing from the pain that now swelled his left arm, Kagan kept rushing, trying not to lose his balance on the slippery sidewalk. He heard someone in the crowd talk about Christmas lights on Canyon Road.

The baby kicked him again.

"Pyotyr, you won't like what I do to you," Andrei swore.

THE BABY WHIMPERED.

"Don't cry," Kagan murmured.

"I'm doing my best to calm him," Meredith insisted.

"I know," Kagan answered gently.

Muscles tightening, he continued to stare out the window toward the falling snow. He couldn't suppress the suspicion that somehow the baby was warning him, as crazy as that seemed.

Did I lose more blood than I realized? Am I so light-headed that I'm imagining things?

The baby became quiet again. But Kagan's muscles didn't relax.

"The rest of the story might not be suitable for Christmas Eve," Kagan said. Hoping to keep the boy intrigued, he added, "Parts of it are what Cole would call gross."

"Then I want to hear it," the boy insisted.

Kagan licked his dry lips. "Okay, but don't say you weren't warned.

"The Magi felt overwhelmed by what the shepherds and Mary had told them. The startling similarities to the story they themselves had told Herod brought them to an extraordinary decision. They violated a primary rule of spycraft and exposed their mission, confessing to Mary that they were foreign operatives pretending to work for Herod.

"'We wanted to drive him insane searching for an imaginary newborn king of the Jews,' they explained. 'But now we find that the story we invented is true. You can't stay here. Soon Herod will wonder why we haven't reported to him. If he learns about your baby from another source, his soldiers will come here and kill you all.'

"What happened next proves that Mary and the shepherds weren't part of a rebel scheme. If they'd been rebels, they'd have realized that the Magi were on their side. They'd have admitted they were rebels and tried to join forces with the Magi to weaken Herod.

"But they didn't. Instead the two groups separated and fled. The Magi chose a new route eastward toward home and acted as decoys. Meanwhile, Joseph hurried with Mary and Jesus southwest toward Egypt. He claimed that he'd had another dream, this one urging him to take his family and run. A spy would argue that the dream was a cover story to protect the Magi, in case Joseph was caught and questioned. It was believable because, as I mentioned, the house of David—to which Joseph belonged—had a tradition of respecting dreams and acting on them. For the same reason, the Magi claimed that they too had experienced a dream that urged them to return home. If questioned, they could maintain that they weren't being disloyal to Herod but were simply responding to the same dictates of their faith that had told them to follow the star.

"Whether Herod would have believed either of these stories is debatable. But at least they had a backup plan.

"Matthew's gospel notes that Joseph, Mary, and Jesus fled by night, something the Magi would have urged them to do, teaching them how to cross the desert in the darkness. The Magi themselves disappear at this point, as good spies should. But the man who told me this version of the Christmas story believed that the Magi eventually rejoined Jesus, Mary, and Joseph in Egypt, teaching them the tricks of tradecraft, such as how to spot signs that they were under surveillance, how to recruit operatives—or what the gospels call disciples—and how to detect double agents.

"The last part makes me certain that Jesus knew Judas would betray him. Indeed, perhaps Jesus *ordered* Judas to betray him in order to fulfill a prophecy. The spy world is a complicated place. But this is a Christmas story, not an Easter one."

Cole interrupted him. "You said you had a theory about why Joseph wasn't with Mary when the Magi talked to her."

"Yes. Given his immense responsibility, Joseph became more a protective agent than a husband and father. While the Magi spoke with Mary, Joseph watched the street outside, on guard against Herod's soldiers. In the future, he would spend increasingly less time with Mary and Jesus because he was always arranging for their security. Like the Magi, he soon disappears from the gospels completely, as a good security officer should. Nowhere in the gospels is he quoted directly. He hovers invisibly in the background."

"But you said there were gross parts," Cole objected.

"Several. They all involve Herod. Contrary to what the Magi hoped, he didn't chase the phantom accounts that popped up here and there all over the country. His erratic behavior didn't destabilize Israel. Instead he did something so disturbing that no one could have predicted it, even taking into account his past actions.

"When Herod realized he'd been tricked, his fury prompted him to send his men to Bethlehem and the other villages in that area. The soldiers obeyed his orders and slaughtered every male child who was two years old or less. Herod couldn't be certain when exactly the new king had been born. By choosing the wide margin of two years, he felt certain he'd eliminated the threat."

"Every boy who was two years old or less?" Cole sounded shocked, yet fascinated. "I heard about that, but I never realized . . . How many boys did he kill?"

"Perhaps as many as a hundred. Tradition says it was a far greater number, but the population of the area that included Bethlehem wasn't large enough for there to be thousands of children. Even so, the mass murder of a hundred children would have *felt* like thousands. The effect on the region was catastrophic.

"If a revolution was indeed being planned, this slaughter of children was so startling that now no one dared move against

Herod. How can you fight someone so psychotic that, in his will, he had made arrangements for several hundred men to have their throats slit at his funeral? He gave that order because he wanted tears to be shed at his death. It didn't matter if the tears were for him or for the slaughtered men. All he cared about was that his subjects would be grief-stricken.

"So, from one point of view, the Magi's plan went terribly wrong. They hoped to destabilize Herod's government, and instead they caused a slaughter. But from another point of view, that mass murder had an unintentional positive effect. By killing every other male child around Bethlehem, Herod insured that the baby Jesus was the only surviving child born when and where the king of peace was prophesied to appear. The census turned out to be crucial. It not only brought Mary and Joseph to Bethlehem to fulfill the prophecy, but it also provided written proof that Jesus was born there.

"As for Herod . . . After the children were slaughtered, a mysterious illness overcame him. An eyewitness reported that the king felt consumed with fire. He convulsed. His legs swelled with water. His bowels developed ulcers. His penis rotted and developed worms."

"Worms on his . . . ewww, *gross*," Cole said.

"I warned you. The historical records say that the king breathed with violent quickness, exuding a terrible odor. His agony lasted for a long time, which I confess gives me satisfaction. After he finally died, the officials in charge of his funeral refused to obey his edict, so no men were murdered when he was buried."

"But what killed him?" the boy asked.

"One theory is that he had chronic kidney disease. Another says he had a raging type of skin cancer. My own belief is that he suffered from what's called the flesh-eating disease. Basically, he was devoured by his own bacteria. It couldn't have happened to a more deserving person. His evil consumed him.

"But what interests me is, how did it happen to him? Was it bad luck? Was it God's will? Or do you suppose a spy had something to do with it, touching Herod with a contaminated cloth that caused the disease? We'll never know. When an espionage mission is successful, we never realize what was actually involved. But I like to think Herod was assassinated with what we now refer to as a biological weapon."

Kagan paused.

"And that's the spy's version of Christmas."

Suddenly the baby cried out.

One moment, it was silent. The next, it wailed as if struck by all the pain and fear in the world, and this time, Kagan was absolutely sure.

"It's beginning," he said.

Part Four

The Child of Peace

"COLE, GET BEHIND the television cabinet! Meredith, take the baby into the laundry room!"

As the baby's wail persisted, Kagan sank from the leather chair and gripped his pistol with two hands, ignoring the pain in his left arm. Although he realized the notion was crazy, every instinct told him that the baby was telling him something, crying out to warn him. He hadn't survived these many years without relying on his instincts, and right now, they were clanging like alarm bells.

Andrei'll come from the front, he reminded himself, pulse racing. *He'll try to distract me while the others attack from the sides. His usual method. The same as at the hotel. He knows I'll expect it, but that doesn't matter. It's the best tactic for this location.*

Nonetheless, while Kagan stared through the window toward the falling snow and the barely visible coyote fence, he didn't see anyone stalking forward.

Maybe I'm imagining things, he hoped. *Maybe they really went away.*

But he knew that if they were watching the house, for sure they could hear the baby now. His ears hurt from the wail.

How can I listen for somebody breaking in?

The wail ended as abruptly as it had begun.

Kagan heard a scraping sound. It came from Meredith desperately pulling the wicker basket into the shadows of the laundry room, where she would try to conceal the baby behind the washer and dryer.

The house became unnaturally still.

Maybe I let my nerves get the better of me, Kagan thought, although he couldn't bring himself to believe it. *It could be that the baby's crying only because he needs his diaper changed.*

At once, Kagan saw a hint of the gate being opened and closed, a figure emerging from the snowfall.

Kagan raised his gun, compensating for the weight of the sound suppressor as he aimed. *Does Andrei think the snow hides him? I can shoot him now. Then I only need to worry about . . .*

But the light above the front door reflected off the snow, revealing that the figure's coat was pale gray and not the black of Andrei's ski jacket. Instead of Andrei's watchman's cap, the man wore a billed cap with earflaps. The figure was Andrei's height, but thin—without Andrei's broad shoulders. When the man came closer, Kagan saw that he had a mustache.

"Meredith?"

"What?"

"Hurry into the living room. Somebody's coming. Does your husband have a mustache? Is this him?"

Kagan heard her footsteps on the brick floor as she scurried through the darkness. Again, he didn't need to remind her to stay low.

"I . . ." She stared out the window. A breath caught in her throat. "Yes. That's Ted."

The front door was to the right of the window. Kagan shifted to the left. Remaining in the shadows, pressing himself close to the window, he stared along the front of the house. He didn't see anyone hiding there. Not that he could see the entire length of the house. But he saw enough to take a chance.

The angle the man followed would lead him to the side door, and Kagan didn't want him entering from that direction. There wasn't a window. Kagan didn't have a way to check for anyone hiding beyond that other door. It would be easy for someone to rush in behind Ted.

"Meredith, open the front door. Tell him to come in *that* way."

She studied Kagan. Even in the shadows, he saw the contour of the swelling bruises on her cheek and the side of her mouth.

"He won't hit you again. I promise."

Meredith nodded, ending her hesitation. She twisted the dead bolt and opened the door. The outside light exposed her. As cold air streamed into the living room, she called out, "Ted, come in. Over here."

"Meredith?" The voice was unsteady, perhaps from alcohol. "Are these footprints out here? The snow almost filled them, but they seem to go toward the house. Did someone show up while I was gone?"

"Get inside," Meredith told him firmly.

"Did I hear a baby cry a few seconds ago?"

"Ted, for heaven's sake, it's *cold*. Get in here."

Ted approached the door.

"Meredith, I'm begging you to forgive me," he said. "The worst thing I ever did in my life was hit you. I'd give anything to take it back. I can't tell you how sorry I am."

Snow flurried in.

Ted took off his gloves and stepped through the door. He cast a shadow from the outside light. "Those footprints—who made them?"

Meredith quickly shut and locked the door.

In a rush, Kagan knocked Ted's legs from under him, dropped him chest first on the floor, pressed the Glock against the back of his head, and told him, "Put your hands behind your neck."

"What's going on? Is that a *gun*?"

"Put your hands behind your neck, and link your fingers."

"Who the—"

Kagan gripped Ted's hair and rapped his forehead on the bricks.

"Ouch!"

"Do what you're told. Meredith, keep looking out the window."

She took Kagan's place in the chair.

Trembling, Ted obeyed Kagan's orders and put his hands behind his neck, linking his fingers. His breath smelled faintly of whiskey, but his speech wasn't slurred, making Kagan think that he hadn't drunk any alcohol in a couple of hours.

"What the hell is going on?"

"Pay attention," Kagan ordered. "Is anybody out there?"

"What do you mean? Who'd be—"

Kagan rapped Ted's forehead on the bricks, harder this time.

"Hey, you're hurting me!"

"That's the whole idea, Ted. *Who's out there?*"

"It's Christmas Eve, for heaven's sake. *Plenty* of people are out there."

"In the lane?"

"No, on Canyon Road."

"I asked about the *lane.*"

"It's deserted. This far from Canyon Road, there aren't many decorations. Why would anybody be in the lane? *Who the hell are you?*"

"Hold still."

Keeping his pistol against the back of Ted's neck, Kagan used his injured arm and painfully searched him. He started at Ted's right ankle, moving up his leg, probing his hips and groin.

"Hey!" Ted objected.

Kagan ignored him, checking his left leg and then the rest of his body. He didn't find any weapons. He did feel a wallet, but not what he was searching for.

"The cell phones," Kagan said. If he could get his hands on one of them, he could call for help. "You left here with two cell phones, yours and Meredith's."

"How did you know that? Why do you care about—"

"Where *are* they?"

"Stolen."

"What?"

"On Canyon Road," Ted answered. "Somebody knocked against me and kept going through the crowd. Then I realized that my coat felt lighter. I reached in my pockets. The cell phones were gone."

"Somebody took the cell phones but not your wallet?"

"In my coat pocket, they were easy to get, but my wallet's under my coat. Meredith, who *is* this guy? How did he get in the house?"

"Shut up while I decide if I believe you," Kagan told him.

"Why wouldn't you believe me? I don't know who you are, buddy, but this is between my wife and me, okay?"

Kagan's instincts told him to let Ted keep talking, on the chance that he might inadvertently say something useful.

Ted looked imploringly at his wife.

"Meredith, I swear I've never been sorrier for anything in my life. Whatever this guy wants, you and I can deal with him. But we can't solve anything if you don't forgive me. After what I did to you, I walked and walked. I felt so bad, I'd have stepped in front of a truck if Canyon Road hadn't been closed to traffic."

"You can come to your hands and knees," Kagan said.

"Everybody was enjoying the carolers and the Christmas lights, but all I wanted was to kill myself." Ted's voice was strained as he glanced around the murky living room. "I don't know what made me notice it, but I saw an old adobe building with a sign that said, 'The Friends.' It struck me as some kind of . . . "

"Come to your knees," Kagan ordered. "Put your hands in your coat pockets."

Ted obeyed, shifting his knees to avoid the folds of his coat, awkwardly stuffing his hands into the pockets. He kept talking the entire time.

"Think about it, Meredith. The one night of the year I surely needed a friend, somebody to straighten me out, and here's this sign."

Kagan remained at the side of the living room, away from the window. "You can stand now."

In the shadows, Ted rose unsteadily, almost losing his balance because his hands were in his coat pockets. He seemed too nervous to stop talking.

"I went in, and there were people sitting on benches along the walls of a big room. Nobody said a word. They had their heads down. I didn't understand until I saw a plaque on the wall: 'The Religious Society of Friends.'"

Ted paused. Again, he looked around the living room.

"They were Quakers, Meredith. I remembered reading in the newspaper that the Quakers have a meeting hall on Canyon Road. The people with their heads down—they were praying. I sat on one of the benches and realized that it had been years since I'd prayed. I'd almost forgotten how to do it, and God knows I had lots to pray for. You. Cole. The strength to quit drinking."

Ted kept looking around the living room. Although Kagan couldn't say why, there was something about Ted's behavior that made him uneasy.

"After a while, they raised their heads and began talking with each other. Their voices were so peaceful. Their faces almost glowed. They looked at me as if I was the most welcome person in the world. One of them brought me a cup of coffee. They didn't pry, but I knew they understood the pain I was in.

"That's where I've been all this time, Meredith, waiting to get sober enough to come home. I couldn't help asking myself where my life was going and what I was doing to you and Cole and . . . Cole? Where *are* you, son? Are you okay?"

"I'm here." Cole's muffled voice came from a corner of the living room.

"Behind the television cabinet? What are you doing *back there*?"

"Hiding."

"From *what*? Did this guy hurt you? If he—"

"No," Meredith insisted, cutting him off. "He didn't hurt us."

"Then somebody tell me what's going on."

"Three men followed me," Kagan said.

"Followed you? What are you talking about?"

"Just shut up and listen. They're tall. Heavy. Tough-looking. In their midforties. One of them has a face like it's been chiseled from a block of wood. Thick eyebrows. A scar on his left cheek. A strong jaw. You're sure you didn't see someone who looks like that out there?"

"I told you, the lane's empty. I didn't see anybody after I left the crowd on Canyon Road. Hey, put the gun down. It's making me nervous."

"It's supposed to. Keep your hands in your pockets."

"It's too dark in here. I can't see your face. Meredith, turn on some lights."

"No," Kagan said.

"Three guys followed you? What do they want?" Ted paused, seeming to focus his thoughts. "I'm sure I heard a baby crying. Where is it?"

Ted stepped to the back of the living room, glancing left and right. His eyes adjusted to the shadows. "Why are all these drawers lying in the hallway outside the bedrooms?"

Kagan followed as Ted moved toward the kitchen. He grabbed Ted's hand when he reached to turn on a light switch.

Ted spoke again, his voice louder. "Why are you boiling—"

"Get back in here." Kagan yanked him into the living room.

Something bothered Kagan about what he'd found or rather *hadn't* found when he'd searched Ted. No weapons. Not surprising. A wallet, but no cell phones. The explanation for the missing cell phones made a degree of sense. Christmas Eve was a perfect time to be a pickpocket. Crowds, confusion. Items in an outside pocket were easy to steal, compared to a wallet underneath the coat.

But there was something else that troubled Kagan. It nagged at the corner of his mind.

Something missing.

Something every man carried in his pants pocket.

"Ted, where are your keys?"

"What?"

"When I searched you, I didn't find any keys. How did you expect to get back in the house?"

"My keys? I didn't . . ." Again Ted paused, as if focusing his thoughts. "I guess I was so drunk, I forgot them."

"No," Meredith said. "You had them in your pocket. You wanted to take the Range Rover, but I insisted that you were too drunk to drive. That's when you hit me. I told you Canyon Road was closed to traffic, and you hit me again. But I guess you finally got the message—because you walked off instead of driving."

"I told you I'm sorry, Meredith. I'll keep saying it as often as I need to. I was wrong. You had every reason to try to keep me from driving. I'll never take another drink, and I swear to God I'll never hit you again."

"Stop changing the subject!" Kagan said. "Where are your keys?"

For a third time, Ted paused. "The pickpocket. He must have taken them. I must have been too drunk to realize it."

"The thief managed to lift two cell phones and your car keys but not your wallet?"

"The keys were in my coat pocket with the cell phones. I remember now. They wouldn't have been hard to get." For a fourth time, Ted paused. Then he spoke again, loudly. "I *know* I heard a baby crying."

"Why are you speaking like that?"

Ted cocked his head.

"The cry seemed to come from . . . the kitchen? No . . . the laundry room."

"Why do you keep pausing?"

"I have no idea what you're talking about. I just want to know what's going on."

"You're giving me a bad feeling, Ted."

"The laundry room."

"A *very* bad feeling. Those men outside—did you lie about them?"

"Why would I—"

"Did they promise they'd let you and Meredith and Cole go free, that they wouldn't hurt you if you helped them?"

"I told you, nobody's out there," Ted protested. The sudden, deeper unsteadiness in his voice made Kagan more apprehensive.

"They're killers, Ted. Whatever they told you isn't true. They have a strict rule about not leaving witnesses."

Meredith turned from crouching near the window. "Ted, dear God, did you lie to us?"

"Of *course* not."

"Are they out there? Are you helping them?"

"I'm not helping anybody," Ted answered, much too fast.

"On your knees again," Kagan ordered.

"My knees?"

"You keep pausing while you talk. Are you listening to someone? Why is your hat still on?"

Kagan kicked the back of Ted's legs and dropped him to his knees. He yanked off Ted's hat. With the earflaps gone, he probed Ted's right ear but found nothing.

"Hey!" Ted objected, trying to twist away.

Kagan probed Ted's left ear, his stomach turning when he found something that blocked it. Sick, he pulled out the ear-bud. "Where's the microphone?"

"Microphone?"

Kagan whacked his gun barrel against the side of Ted's forehead. "You stupid fool, give me the damned microphone!"

Ted groaned, raising a hand to his head.

"The microphone!" Kagan hit him again with the gun barrel. "Where is it?"

"Under my coat collar."

Kagan found it and pulled it free. "Where's the transmitter?"

"In one of my gloves. When you knocked me down, I shoved it under that chair."

Grabbing for it, Kagan shouted, "Meredith, you know where to go. Hurry. Cole, he told them you're hiding behind the television cabinet. You'll need to find another spot."

"But they promised they wouldn't hurt us!" Ted insisted, his voice rising. "I'd never put my son in danger!"

"That's exactly what you did."

"No! All I care about is protecting my family. Meredith, I was only trying to help you and Cole. Surely you understand that."

"Pay attention," Kagan demanded. "Who are you going to believe? Your wife and son, who trust me, or those men outside, who'll do anything to get their hands on the baby? I promise you, they won't think twice about killing us all. They never leave witnesses."

"All I wanted was—"

"For God's sake, shut up and help your family!"

CROUCHING IN THE living room, Kagan listened as Meredith hurried toward the laundry room, where she'd hidden the baby.

He had no idea what new hiding place Cole had chosen, and he didn't dare ask, aware that Andrei would hear through the microphone he'd taken from Brody. He was about to shut off the transmitter or relieve his anger by hurling the microphone onto the brick floor and smashing it, but suddenly he realized he had a use for it.

He shoved the earbud into his left ear and spoke into the microphone. "Andrei?"

"Regrets, my friend?" The voice sounded bitter. "I warned you how this would end."

Instinctively, Kagan directed his words toward the front window.

"There are computers in the house. I e-mailed for help. The police are on their way."

"No, Pyotyr. When I rehearsed things with my not-so-good spy, he told me his computers have password locks."

"Password locks," Kagan repeated, staring at Ted.

Ted seemed paralyzed by confusion. Abruptly, he murmured, "I'll fix that." He crawled across the living room, squirmed over the drawers at the end of the hallway, and entered his office.

"Give me the package, and my offer still holds," Andrei's acid voice said through the earbud. "You can walk away."

"Why don't I believe you?" Kagan said into the microphone.

"Then consider *this*. Your foolishness has involved other people. You're responsible for everything that happens to the family in there. Their deaths will be your fault."

Kagan couldn't help glancing behind him: first toward the shadows of the laundry room, where Meredith hid with the baby, and then toward a glow in Ted's office, presumably caused by a computer screen. He heard Ted's fingers clicking at a keyboard.

Where's Cole? he wondered.

"But if you give me the package," Andrei's voice said, "I'll let the family live."

"Even though they're witnesses?"

"Only the man saw us. But I'll make an exception and allow him to live, along with his wife and son. We'll be out of Santa Fe before the police get organized. I don't risk much by letting the family survive. It's my gesture to you, Pyotyr, because I valued your friendship, even though you didn't value mine. Give me the package. Accept your punishment. Since you apparently have a conscience, at least you'll know that others won't suffer because of you."

"It's a baby, Andrei. Not a package. If I do as you ask, what happens to him?"

"Our clients will keep it, to use it to pressure Hassan into rejecting his cause and going back to being a doctor. That's a better way than assassinating him and turning him into a martyr. In his speeches, Hassan promises his followers that he'll be tireless in his pursuit of a lasting peace. When he swears, 'I'll never let you down,' thousands flock to him. If he quits, his followers will be so disillusioned that his cause will wither."

"And a year from now? Two years from now? What happens to the child then?" Kagan demanded.

"Hassan and his wife will be allowed occasional secret visits. There's a birthmark on its left heel."

"Yes. Shaped like a rose."

"Proof that it's still alive, that there hasn't been a substitution. To keep anything from happening to it, Hassan and his wife won't dare to take up the cause again."

"You keep calling the baby 'it.' Not 'it,' Andrei. *He*. A person."

"Pyotyr, you know there are only objects. If you'd remembered that, you wouldn't be having this problem. What's your real name?"

Kagan ignored the question. He had an urgent one of his own.

"Hassan's enemies, will they raise his child?"

"Yes. Until he's old enough to be trained as a suicide bomber."

The statement felt like a blow to Kagan's stomach. Something in him went numb. Only after a moment did he realize that Andrei had referred to the child as "he," not "it."

"What's your real name?" Andrei repeated.

Train him to be a suicide bomber? Kagan felt sickened, unable to speak.

Ted crawled from his office and reached Kagan, who tapped the microphone against his leg to prevent Andrei from hearing what Ted whispered.

"I have phone capability on my computers, but when I tried the Santa Fe police, all I got was a busy signal. The snow must have caused a lot of accidents. I sent an e-mail to people I know in Santa Fe, telling them to contact the police and get a SWAT team here."

Kagan nodded, doing his best to look optimistic. Still, he couldn't help thinking, *It's Christmas Eve. Is this the one night of the year when people won't check their e-mail? Or will their phone calls only jam the 911 phone circuits more? How many hours might it take before the police arrive?*

The glow from Ted's office made him feel exposed. He whispered to Ted. "The light from your monitors. Shut them off."

Immediately, he stopped tapping the microphone and said to it, "My real name? It's what I told you. It's Pyotyr. I didn't lie about everything. Our friendship's real."

"Of course. And your *last* name?" Andrei's voice asked.

"You know I won't tell you that. I need to protect my family."

"Your family?" Andrei sounded indignant. "You mean you have a wife, and you didn't tell me?"

"No! How could I work undercover this long and be married? Don't you think I want a wife and children like *you* do? Don't you think I *envy* you? My mother and father. *They're* my family."

Kagan said it with a subdued wave of grief. His parents were, in fact, dead—the victims of a drunk driver who'd hit their car head-on two years earlier. But he needed to try to make Andrei relate to him as a person, and parents who were still alive gave him a sympathetic reason not to reveal his last name.

"And you work for American intelligence?"

"Yes."

"You admit it. Finally, some truth."

"Andrei, remember the day we drove down to the gun dealer in Maryland to pick up that load of weapons the Pakhan wanted? We made the dealer add our Glocks as a bonus. We spent the afternoon on the firing range, testing who's a better shot."

"And my Glock will be the gun that kills you."

"Listen to me. In the last few years, I can't recall a better afternoon," Kagan said. He concentrated on the kitchen door, ready to shoot if someone charged in. "I *am* your friend, Andrei. I was honored to be invited to your home. I felt privileged to be with your wife and daughters. They're the family I never had. Remember when I saved your life in Colombia?"

"Don't make too much of that, Pyotyr."

Kagan shifted his attention to the shadows in the hallway, listening for someone breaking in.

"That drug lord was seriously pissed off when he realized the Soviet-era submarine you'd sold him would sink the first time he tried to use it to smuggle cocaine into the United States. I'm the one who spotted the ambush in that parking garage. You were ahead of me and the other men. I could have left you and run like the others did. But I got you out of there when no one else tried."

"And as thanks, I'll make your death instantaneous."

"Some things can't be faked, Andrei. Our friendship is one of them. You'd have sensed immediately if I was playing a game. I never told my controllers about anything that you were personally involved in. I never did anything that put you at risk."

"Except when you stole the baby."

Kagan noticed that Andrei said "the baby" and not "the package." That gave him a reason to hope.

"No one is more ruthless than our clients," Andrei insisted. "If I don't deliver what they paid us to get, they'll never stop hunting me. The Pakhan, too, will never stop hunting me."

"There's an alternative!" Kagan kept pacing, checking the kitchen door and the hallway.

"I can't imagine what it could be."

"Come over to *my* side."

"*Your* side?"

"Work for us."

"Defect?" Andrei made the concept sound outrageous.

"Just pretend it's the Cold War."

"Join American intelligence? And you make this proposal on a radio frequency to which my comrades are listening. Is *this* the quality of tradecraft your controllers taught you?"

"It's the only way I have of talking with you! Listen to me, Andrei. Working for *my* side is better than stealing babies. Don't you have a personal low, a point beyond which you'd despise yourself? Isn't there ever a time when you feel ashamed? Worse than that? Disgusted?"

Andrei fell silent.

"That's what I've been feeling for a very long time," Kagan continued. "Self-disgust."

"I do what's necessary for business," Andrei's voice replied.

"But there are other ways to earn a living. Your wife doesn't have any idea how many people you've killed to pay for that nice house near the beach. Your daughters don't know how much blood it took to earn their tuition at that wonderful private school they attend. How do you suppose they'd react if they found out what you really are? One day, government agents will pound on your door. Or else one night, rival gangsters will go to your home and—"

"Shut up!"

"Andrei, you once said we didn't have a choice about our lives. Well, now I'm giving you a chance to take control. Join me. Wouldn't it be great to tell your wife and daughters the truth about what you do, and to know it's honorable? My people will relocate them," Kagan said into the microphone. "You'll all receive new identities. Your wife and daughters will be protected. You won't need to be afraid for them."

Kagan hoped it was true. He couldn't help recalling the fear with which his parents and he had lived, despite the best promises of the State Department.

"You'll earn an honest salary, doing good for a change," Kagan said. "Wouldn't it feel wonderful to give the child of peace a chance to fulfill his destiny?"

"Destiny?" Andrei mocked. "You sound like a politician."

"When I was running from you tonight, I felt as if the baby was trying to communicate with me, to tell me where to go and warn me when you were close."

"Your wound made you hallucinate."

"But I believe the baby *does* have a destiny, Andrei. His father's amazing: a powerful, inspiring leader who preaches hope instead of hate. Imagine how much more amazing his son can be. Maybe *our* destiny is to guarantee that he fulfills *his*. Why don't we make sure the baby gets back to his parents?"

"Then the clients and the Pakhan would hunt down *both* of us. Neither our deaths nor those of my family would be quick."

"That won't happen if we hunt them first, Andrei. We can make them sorry they ever thought of raising the baby to be a suicide bomber. Who was the monster who had *that* idea? How's that for somebody's personal low? Let's show them we're better than that. Let's show them we're human beings."

Kagan paused, turning his head toward the outside entrance to the kitchen. *Did I hear something? A key being slid into a lock?*

Again, he tapped the microphone against his leg so that Andrei couldn't hear what he whispered to Ted.

"There's a pot of boiling water on the stove. Put it on top of the microwave. When I shout, 'Now,' push the microwave's start button. The timer's already set."

Kagan was close enough that, even in the shadows, he saw Ted's forehead tighten in confusion.

"I don't have time to explain, Ted. For Meredith and Cole, just do it. They're depending on you."

Ted hesitated, then surprised him by nodding.

"Whatever you want. I've got a hell of a lot to make up for." Staying low, Ted hurried into the kitchen.

Kagan stopped tapping the microphone against his leg. He clipped it to his shirt. "Andrei, are you still there? The snow must be interfering with the radio transmission. All I heard was interference."

"I'm afraid it's a little late for me to pretend to be a human being, Pyotyr," Andrei's voice responded. "Is the baby somewhere safe?"

Again, Kagan noted that Andrei said "the baby" and not "the package." He kept hoping he'd gotten through to him.

"Yes. He's somewhere safe."

"I think Ted was right when he said the laundry room. *Merry Christmas.*"

There was something about the firmness with which Andrei said the last two words.

Abruptly, the baby cried out in the laundry room.

BULLETS PUNCHED holes in the front window, spraying shards of glass into the living room.

The shots were silent. By contrast, the crash of the glass and the impact of the bullets against the back wall were shockingly loud, but not so loud that Kagan didn't hear a window shatter in the master bedroom.

Someone was breaking in.

They'll come from three directions.

"Now, Ted! Now!" he yelled. "Turn it on!"

In spite of the baby's wail, he heard the hum of the microwave. As Ted stayed low and rushed back into the living room, a crackling sound came from the kitchen. Kagan saw periodic flashes through the archway, the crumpled tinfoil in the microwave arcing like miniature lightning.

The door to the kitchen banged open. A hunched silhouette charged in, shooting at everything before him, his bullets walloping walls and cupboards, the sound-suppressed shots themselves inaudible in the commotion.

Suddenly, a loud *crack* was accompanied by a blinding glare. In the microwave, the heated glue burst from its plastic tube, the arcs from the tinfoil igniting its highly volatile vapor.

As the microwave exploded in a fireball, Kagan saw the oven door rocket toward the gunman at the same time that the pot of scalding water catapulted off the oven, spraying over him.

Smoke from the explosion filled the kitchen. Hearing screams, Kagan ran through the archway, saw a figure writhing in agony on the floor, and shot him twice in the head. The gunman was Yakov. In the confines of the kitchen, Kagan's sound-suppressed shots made noises like muted snaps from a nail gun.

He rushed to the kitchen door, slammed it shut, and twisted the lock.

The smoke thickened. He saw flames licking the cupboard above where the fireball had erupted from the microwave.

"Are you all right?" Ted yelled from the living room. His voice sounded farther away because Kagan's ears rang from the explosion.

"The kitchen's on fire!" Kagan shouted back.

Their voices overlapped as Ted yelled, "Someone's in the master bedroom! I heard something falling!"

Eyes watering from the smoke, Kagan crouched next to the archway that opened into the living room. He wiped his sleeve across his eyes and aimed along the corridor that led to the other end of the house.

Behind him, the flames grew. Now the smoke reflected it, the illumination making him feel exposed.

Air brushed past his head.

Again.

Again.

Bullets. Someone was shooting from the end of the corridor, the noise barely audible. The gunman's sound suppressor hid the muzzle flashes, too, making it difficult for Kagan to judge exactly where to aim.

He squeezed off two quick shots toward the master bedroom. He hated to use the ammunition on a target he couldn't see, but he needed to make the gunman stay in the bedroom.

"Ted, you'll soon hear another explosion! When it happens, don't hesitate! Run into the kitchen and try to put out the fire!"

Ted didn't answer.

"Ted!" Kagan shouted.

"He heard what you told me to do! He'll wait for me to run! He'll shoot when he sees me in the light from the fire!"

"Just trust me! Do what I say!"

Again, Ted didn't answer.

The only sound was the crackle of the flames growing on the cupboard door.

Kagan tried desperately not to cough. He felt another streak of air sweep past him and shot toward the end of the corridor.

Simultaneously, three bullets shattered more glass in the living room window. Someone—probably Andrei—was shooting from the front.

The baby wailed.

"Ted!" Kagan yelled. "The only way Meredith and the baby can leave the laundry room is through the kitchen! You've got to put out the fire before they're trapped!"

"I promised I'll do whatever you want! Just tell me when!"

"Get ready!"

Kagan squeezed the trigger again and again. His bullets were directed toward the floor at the end of the hallway, toward the pressurized cans of hair spray and shaving soap he'd placed there. They were thirty yards away, difficult targets even in daylight. As the fire grew behind him, all he could do was keep shooting.

He assumed that the gunman, having been warned, would duck back from the master bedroom's doorway and take cover. That—along with the bursting cans—should provide Ted the protection he needed to get into the kitchen, Kagan hoped.

Taking one more shot, he flinched as a sharp *bang* assaulted his ears. A can exploded, spraying the end of the hallway with chunks of metal and pressurized liquid.

"Now, Ted! Now!"

But Ted was already in motion, racing past him into the kitchen. He stumbled over Yakov's corpse, grabbed the kitchen table to catch his balance, and veered toward the sink. The force of his movement parted the smoke and brightened the flames that wavered up the cupboard next to the kitchen door.

Almost out of ammunition, Kagan thought.

He heard water running in the sink, the clatter of a saucepan, water splashing into it. Steam hissed as Ted hurled the water against the burning cupboard.

The light from the flames diminished.

Again, water splashed into the saucepan. Again, Ted hurled it against the cupboard.

"It's out!" he yelled.

The thickening shadows told Kagan the same thing.

Yakov's gun, he thought. *If I can reach it . . .*

He risked switching his gaze from the hallway and focused on the corpse next to him. But the bright flames had hurt his night vision, and he couldn't adapt to the dark again to see the gun.

More bullets snapped past him, but this time they were directed behind him, toward the floor. Kagan realized that the flames must have illuminated the pressurized cans he'd placed next to the kitchen door. The gunman was imitating his tactic.

"Ted, get over by the sink!"

The sharp *bang* with which one of the cans exploded felt like hands slapping Kagan's ears.

In agony, Kagan tried to recover from the shock. Aiming along the hallway, he saw a figure lunge from the master bedroom.

He knows I'm down to my last few rounds!

The gunman had Mikhail's bulky silhouette. He must have put in a fresh magazine, Kagan realized, because he kept shooting as if he had an endless supply of ammunition.

Having been warned about the drawers that lay on the floor, Mikhail veered this way and that. The zigzag movement confused Kagan's aim as Mikhail kept shooting.

Kagan fired once, twice, but then his gun was useless, its slide locking back, its magazine empty. Certain that he was about to die, he rolled frantically toward Yakov's body next to him, searching for the gun. But his wounded arm was so stiff that it restricted his movement.

Doubly certain that he would die, he felt a bullet strike the brick floor, spraying fragments over him.

He kept pawing for Yakov's gun but couldn't find it.

Without warning, Mikhail stumbled, sprawling face-down onto a drawer. Something about the way he fell struck Kagan as strange, but there wasn't time to think about it as he unclipped the knife from his pocket and surged up.

The hook on the back of the knife levered against his pocket and pulled the blade open.

Charging, he saw Mikhail's shadowy figure peer up from the floor and raise his pistol. Kagan slashed the back of Mikhail's wrist, causing him to drop the gun. But as Kagan slashed again, Mikhail used his uninjured hand to grab his ankle and yank him off balance.

Kagan fell heavily.

When he hit the floor, he crunched across broken glass, managing to come to his feet at the same moment that Mikhail rose and dove forward. Despite their injured arms, they grappled viciously, sliding on the shards of glass. Kagan fought to stab his opponent, while Mikhail struggled to get the knife away from him.

Kagan's heart sped so wildly that the precise movements necessary for martial-arts combat became impossible. He and Mikhail were like two large animals, colliding with each other.

Mikhail was heavier, able to make his weight a weapon. He used his uninjured hand to squeeze Kagan's knife wrist, spinning him. Then he curled his blood-slick arm around Kagan's neck, strangling him from behind. Kagan felt increasing pressure against his larynx.

Something crashed.

Andrei's breaking through the front window! Kagan thought.

But the crash was accompanied by a blow from behind that sent Mikhail lurching forward.

Ted hit him with something!

In a frenzy, Kagan squirmed free of Mikhail's grip. He tried to slice with the blade, but again Mikhail grabbed that wrist. The force of their struggle knocked Kagan against the back wall of the corridor. His head smashed the glass of a picture hanging there.

Dizzy from the impact, he tried to knee Mikhail in the groin but succeeded only in striking a thigh. As the Russian pinned him against the wall, straining to get the knife away from him, Kagan stomped down hard on a foot and heard a groan. To the right, he sensed the open door to Ted's office and used all his strength to pivot with Mikhail, thrusting him through the doorway.

The trip cord caught behind Mikhail's ankles. Kagan added to the Russian's backward momentum by shoving. When they hit the floor, Kagan was on top, his impact knocking the air from Mikhail's lungs. The Russian's grip loosened enough for Kagan to yank his knife hand free.

Screaming with fury, he plunged the blade into Mikhail's throat, all the way to the handle, and felt the Russian thrash. He worked the knife back and forth, widening the hole, grating against bone, feeling the hot blood gush over his fingers. Mikhail's mouth gaped in a desperate effort to breathe.

His arms fought to push Kagan away. He gasped, the blood causing a rattle in his throat. His arms lost strength. Kagan kept twisting the knife. At last, Mikhail's hands fell away, trembled, and lay still.

Only then did Kagan let go of the knife. *Andrei!* he thought frantically.

Dizzy from his frenzied breathing, he scrambled toward where Mikhail had dropped his pistol. He grabbed the gun, hurried into the living room, crouched, and aimed toward the bullet holes in the front window. Huge chunks of glass had fallen into the room. The snow was drifting in.

Where was Andrei?

Kagan's ears rang painfully. From the laundry room, the baby kept crying, its wail seeming to come through cotton batting.

But Kagan noticed something odd—inexplicably, the window was broken only at the top half. Every bullet had been directed upward, where the least possible harm would result.

What the . . . ?

"Look out!" Ted shouted behind him.

Spinning, Kagan saw a dark figure lurch from the office. Mikhail's throat gaped, wheezing, spewing blood. The knife was no longer embedded there. It was in his hand, and as he thrust the blade toward Kagan, Ted surged from the kitchen, crashing into him. The impact sent Ted and Mikhail toppling onto the floor. Raging, Mikhail swung the knife at Ted, who kicked and fought to squirm away.

The knife grazed Ted's cheek, making him groan. But he was far enough away that Kagan could shoot without fear of hitting him. He put two bullets behind Mikhail's right ear, and when the Russian collapsed, this time Kagan had no doubt that he was dead.

Andrei. Where's Andrei?

Kagan whirled again toward the front window.

HE WAS DRENCHED in sweat. His breathing was frantic. He knew that barely two minutes had elapsed, but the intensity of the fight had made the passage of time seem much longer.

The baby kept wailing. Then suddenly, it stopped.

At once, Kagan heard Andrei's voice, but this time, it didn't come from the radio's earbud. Instead it came faintly from the area outside the house. Although Kagan had the sense that Andrei was shouting, the explosions had traumatized his ears enough that he had to strain to hear what was being said.

"Pyotyr!" the voice called. "Don't say a word! Shut off your radio transmitter!"

Wary, Kagan didn't respond.

"Do you hear me?" Andrei shouted. "Shut off the transmitter!"

What's he up to? Kagan wondered. Tense, he did as he was asked.

"Okay, it's off!" Kagan's words seemed to come from inside a tunnel.

"I figured you were the one who survived. Otherwise, Yakov or Mikhail would have opened the door."

"It's nice to know you have confidence in me."

"More than you can imagine," Andrei said. "By the way, I shut off *my* radio transmitter also. The clients and the Pakhan can't hear us."

"What are you doing?" Kagan aimed toward the half-broken window. More snow flurried through it. "All your shots were aimed high. If you'd continued the attack from the front, I'd have been killed."

"You mentioned destiny. I figured I'd let Mikhail and Yakov decide it for me. If they won, then the child was meant to be delivered to our clients."

"I thought you didn't believe in destiny." Kagan kept aiming through the window.

"Of course I do. I'm Russian."

"Tell me why you held back."

"Things happened tonight, Pyotyr."

"Yeah, it was a busy Christmas Eve."

"The Pakhan called me certain names," Andrei said.

"Names?"

"Hooyesos. Govnosos. Kachok. Koshkayob."

"That's a lot of disrespect."

"He sided with the clients against me. He threatened me. Worse, he threatened my family."

"And nobody threatens your family."

"Believe it. Pyotyr, suppose I do defect. Where do you think I should ask for my wife and daughters to be relocated? You know Anna. What would she like?"

"Considering tonight's weather, I think someplace warm." Kagan was reminded of why his parents had chosen Miami.

"Or perhaps she's tired of living near water and would enjoy a change of scenery."

"That's something you'll need to discuss with her."

"As soon as we finish here," Andrei said from the front of the house. "You and I have hunting to do. If I'm going to switch sides, I can't leave my enemies alive to come after me and my family."

Kagan heard a voice behind him. It belonged to Ted, who was saying something urgently. Then Kagan realized that Ted wasn't speaking to anyone in the house, and that he'd done something remarkable.

"Andrei," he said through the shattered window, "Ted turned out to have more nerve than we imagined. He risked his life to save his wife and son. Now he searched one of the bodies to get a cell phone. He's talking to the police. How he got through I'll never know. But he did. I mention that in case you have a surprise planned."

"You think I'm not telling the truth?"

"I think that if this is a trick to grab the baby, you've got less than five minutes to make your move."

"What kind of friends don't trust each other?" Andrei chided. "Actually, you're the one who has less than five minutes. If we're going to make this work, we need to get out of here right away. When I gave Yakov the key to the house, I kept the car keys. I used them a few minutes ago to back the Range Rover out of the garage."

"I don't hear it."

"I wouldn't expect you to, given what those explosions must have done to your ears. What caused them?"

"The big one was a microwave I blew up."

"Always resourceful. I'm sure Yakov and Mikhail were startled enough to lose their momentum."

"For certain, Yakov did."

"The bastard shouldn't have run away when that drug lord tried to kill me in Colombia. Pyotyr, make up your mind. If you want me to defect, you need to get out here and help me do what's necessary."

The snowfall was now so thick that Kagan could hardly see anything beyond the window. *Is he trying to fool me into showing myself?* he wondered.

"Andrei, do you know what Santa Fe means?"

"Someone in the crowd mentioned it tonight. Holy Faith."

"I guess it's time to have some faith of my own."

Anything for the baby, Kagan thought. *I need to keep Andrei occupied. I need to keep him away from the house.*

"All right, I'm coming out."

He turned toward Ted, who lowered the cell phone and told him, "A SWAT team and an ambulance are on the way."

"Thank God," Meredith said. She stepped from the laundry room, appearing through the smoke that lingered in the kitchen. The lights outside provided enough illumination to show Kagan that she held the baby.

"Are you all right?" he asked.

"Scared. Sick." She glanced nervously toward Yakov's body, then quickly away.

"And the baby?"

"He isn't hurt."

Kagan felt a momentary relief that was suddenly broken.

"Wait a minute. Where's Cole?"

"Cole?" Ted's voice was stark. "Where are you, son?"

"Cole?" Meredith looked around desperately.

Kagan almost panicked, fearing that the boy had been shot, but then he heard a faint voice.

"I'm here," Cole said. He limped from the shadowy hallway. Dragging his baseball bat, he made his way unsteadily among the drawers on the floor. Even in the shadows, Mikhail's body was obvious.

It made Cole stop.

"Cole, can you see me?" Ted asked. "Keep your eyes on me. Don't look down, son. I'm coming to get you."

Broken glass scraped under Ted's shoes as he walked over. He picked up his son and lifted him over the corpse.

When Ted set him down, Kagan put a reassuring hand on Cole's shoulder. He'd been puzzled by something that had happened during the gunfight, but now he understood.

"Cole, when I told you to find a new hiding place, where did you go?" Kagan asked. "You came from the hallway. Were you in the bathroom?"

"Yes." Cole sounded as if he was in shock. "I was lying in the bathtub."

"The second man charged from the master bedroom," Kagan continued. "But I was out of ammunition. The only thing that gave me time to grab my knife was that he tripped."

"Of course," Meredith said. "He tripped on one of the drawers you set down."

"No, he knew about the drawers," Kagan told her. "And he was moving confidently. I don't think it was a drawer that tripped him."

"Then what happened?" Ted asked. "Why did he fall?"

"You'd better ask Cole."

"I don't understand. What are you talking about?"

"Tell them, Cole," Kagan said. "Your mother and father should know how brave you are."

"Brave?" Ted sounded baffled.

The boy hesitated. "I had to help. With all the noise, the man didn't hear me crawl out of the bathtub. When he ran past, I stuck out my bat."

"*You* tripped him?" Meredith asked in amazement.

Cole fidgeted with the baseball bat. "I didn't know what else to do."

Meredith spoke softly. "My dear brave boy."

"He's more than a boy," Kagan said.

"I hear sirens," Cole said, looking up.

With little time remaining, Kagan stepped toward Meredith and the baby she held. He put a finger on the tiny forehead.

"The child of peace? Lord, I hope so. Grow strong and healthy, little guy. Make me believe that it's possible to have peace on earth and goodwill to all."

Andrei yelled from outside. There was nervousness in his voice now. "The sirens, Pyotyr."

Kagan looked at Ted.

"Your left cheek's bleeding."

"What?" Ted jerked a hand to his face and touched the blood.

"Might have been flying glass or—"

"No. The knife did it."

"It's deep. I'm afraid you'll have a scar."

"That's good."

"I don't understand."

"It'll remind me of what I almost lost." Ted turned toward Meredith and Cole.

Kagan did the same. "Meredith, did anyone ever tell you how beautiful you are?"

She glanced down in embarrassment. If the lights had been on, Kagan was sure he'd have seen her blushing.

"Ted, don't you think she's beautiful?"

"Very much."

"Tell her every day."

Kagan went into the kitchen and pulled on his parka, concealing Mikhail's blood that covered his shirt. He shoved Mikhail's gun and his own Glock into the right pocket of the coat. He picked up Yakov's gun and reloaded it with a remaining magazine he found on the corpse.

"Meredith, tell the police everything that happened. Don't hold anything back. You don't know anything that can harm me. Just say the truth. And Cole, don't forget the story about the Magi."

"The spy's version of Christmas." The boy sounded dazed.

"What story is that?" Ted asked.

"Your son will tell you."

"Pyotyr!" Andrei's voice warned from outside. "The police! We don't have much time!"

"Ted, walk with me." They moved to the front door.

"When I fought with the second man, I felt something crash against him. Did you hit him from behind?" Kagan asked.

"With a lamp." Blood dripped from Ted's cheek.

"There might be hope for you yet. Have you ever fired a gun?"

"No."

"You point the barrel and pull the trigger. There are refinements, but basically that's it."

"Is there a reason you want me to know this?"

"Take this gun. The man you spoke to, the one with the creased face and the thick eyebrows, if he tries to come inside the house, don't let him."

"You think he might break his word? You think you might be walking into a trap?"

"It's been known to happen." Kagan looked behind him. "Cole, what's a major rule of being a spy?"

Cole spoke numbly. "Don't take anything for granted."

"What's another rule?"

"Always have a backup plan."

"I'm proud of you." Kagan studied the boy's father. "Ted, can I rely on you to stop that man if he tries to get inside?"

"Anything to protect my family."

"Keep remembering that. To protect your family."

"You have my word."

"If you ever forget, if you ever hurt your wife and son, one day I'll come back and remind you of this conversation."

"You won't need to."

Ted held out his hand.

Kagan shook it, noting that, despite everything that had happened, Ted's grip was firm.

"I believe you."

At the front door, he looked back at the baby snuggling contentedly in Meredith's arms.

Are you sending me another sign? he wondered. *That everything's going to be okay?*

"Enjoy your roses, Meredith."

"Thank you for saving our lives."

"No need to thank me. I'm the one who put you in danger. We wouldn't be alive if all of you hadn't been strong." Kagan pointed toward Cole. "I've known some professionals who aren't as dependable."

"Well, thank you anyway," she said, "for keeping your promise." She looked at Ted and then back at Kagan. "You gave me a Christmas present."

As Kagan gathered his resolve and reached for the doorknob, she added, "You never told me your name. The man outside called you 'Pyotyr.' Does that mean 'Peter'? Is that your name?"

"That's what he calls me."

Meredith thought about it and nodded. "I understand. Whoever you are," she replied, "Merry Christmas."

KAGAN OPENED the door and exposed himself to the overhead lights. If Andrei meant to shoot him, this was his chance.

But nothing happened.

Everything's an act of faith, he thought. Shivering, he stepped from the house and walked through the falling snow toward the gate. He heard the faint rumble of an engine. As he reached the lane, he saw the dark shape of a Range Rover.

When I open the door, that's when it'll happen, Kagan thought, snow pelting him.

The passenger window descended.

"Pyotyr, you promised you'd help! I can't defect if the clients and the Pakhan are hunting me and my family. The last time they'll be together is tonight! This is my only chance."

It might be a trick, Kagan thought. *But at least I saved the child.*

"From now on, there won't be any lies," he said, hanging back. "My real name isn't Pyotyr."

"Imagine that. What a surprise."

"It's Paul." Kagan stepped toward the door. He hoped that his tone made Andrei realize he was telling the truth.

"I'll never get used to calling you that."

"Then keep calling me 'Pyotyr.'"

"Are you thinking about shooting me through the window?" Andrei asked.

"Actually, I was thinking about you and me doing some good," Kagan replied.

His hearing had improved sufficiently for him to realize that the sirens were nearer than he liked.

"Doing some good?" Andrei thought about it and shrugged. "Why not? It's better than stealing babies."

When Kagan opened the passenger door, he saw that both of Andrei's hands were placed firmly on the steering wheel.

"Now's the time, if you want to shoot me," Andrei said. "I'm helpless."

Kagan got in from the cold.

"I can't imagine you ever being helpless." Kagan shut the door.

Andrei put the Range Rover in gear and drove along the lane. The deep snow crunched under the high vehicle's tires. A short time later, he turned right onto Canyon Road, where a few cars were now in motion.

"Do you hear that?" Andrei asked.

Kagan strained to listen.

"The sirens?"

"The cathedral bells," Andrei said. "It's midnight."

"Christmas."

The word made Kagan think of his dead parents and the Christmases he would never spend with them.

"Look behind us," Andrei said.

Kagan turned. The Range Rover's window had a heating element that melted the snow landing on it. In the distance, he saw the hazy red and blue flashing lights of police cars doing their best to move up Canyon Road. The flashes reminded him of lights on a Christmas tree. Then the snowfall strengthened, obscuring them.

When Andrei steered left onto another road, the Range Rover's tire tracks blended with others. He drove over a small bridge, reached a stop sign, waited for the lights of a car to go past, and followed it to the left. A few seconds later, the lights of another car came along the street behind them.

Andrei peered into the rearview mirror. "They'll be looking for a blue Range Rover. Downtown's only a couple of blocks away. We'll find a parking lot and abandon the car. It shouldn't be hard to find something else to steal. No one'll notice it's gone until the morning."

"Sounds like a plan."

Andrei pointed at twinkling lights on houses they passed. "Where I grew up, there wasn't any such thing as Christmas. After the Soviet Union collapsed and I snuck into the United States, I was amazed by all the decorations."

"Only the decorations? What about the Christmas spirit?"

"Since you appear to have developed a conscience, maybe you can teach me."

"You already have a conscience," Kagan said.

"Don't make me regret it."

Andrei reached for something under his ski jacket. For a moment, Kagan feared that Andrei had fooled him and was drawing a gun. He almost lunged to defend himself. But then he realized that Andrei was turning on the radio transmitter that was hooked to his belt.

"This is Melchior," Andrei said to the microphone on his coat. "I have the package." He paused, listening to his earbud as he drove through the slow-moving traffic. "It's safe and ready for delivery. The *mudak* is no longer in business."

Andrei listened some more.

"Yes, it was a pathetic attempt to persuade me to join his corporation. In the end, I made sure he realized what a fool he was. The only person I'm loyal to is you." Again, Andrei listened. "The main thing is, I corrected my mistake. Tell the clients I meant what I said. When I deliver the package, I want an apology, along with a bonus. We'll be there in half an hour. Oh, and tell room service to deliver vodka for us."

Andrei pressed a button on the transmitter, turning it off.

"A half hour. That gives us time to prepare."

"*Mudak*. That's a tough thing to call me," Kagan said.

"It's better than what the Pakhan called *me*. Is your name truly Paul?"

"I'm trusting you with it."

"Paul." Andrei tested the name. "No, it won't do. Pyotyr, after you help me defect, perhaps you can spend next Christmas with me and my family."

"It'll be a pleasure to see them again."

The baby's safe, Kagan kept thinking. *Nothing else matters. I saved the baby. I can bear sitting here, trying to make jokes with Andrei, while we drive to a gunfight. I can tolerate helping him whatever way he wants. As long as the baby's safe.*

"Perhaps here in Santa Fe. Perhaps this is where Anna and the girls would enjoy living," Andrei said.

"A little too close to business, don't you think?"

"I know how to blend."

"You do indeed," Kagan admitted.

"The mountains. The light. The quiet. There are many things here they'd enjoy."

"Quiet's a good thing," Kagan agreed.

Thank God the baby's safe, he kept thinking. His ears recovered sufficiently that he could now hear the cathedral bells.

"Do you have enough ammunition?" Andrei asked.

"My Glock's empty. I have a partially full magazine in Mikhail's pistol."

"Here's a spare magazine for the Glock."

Kagan watched warily as Andrei reached into his ski jacket. But when his hand came out, it held only the magazine he'd promised.

"Pyotyr, maybe you can explain something to me."

"Whatever you want to know. I told you that from now on, I'll be completely honest."

"Have you seen the movie *It's a Wonderful Life*?"

Kagan overcame his confusion and answered, "Many times. My parents watched it every year."

"I'm surprised you could watch it even once. It mystifies me. Why do people like it so much? Don't you think that fat angel looks stupid? And what's with James Stewart? He's too skinny. He should have stuffed himself with more Christmas dinners."

"If he stuffed himself, he'd look just like the angel," Kagan said.

"I didn't say he should stuff himself *that* much. But the character he played was so trusting, it's a wonder he wasn't cheated out of everything he owned."

"Someone needs to make sure that doesn't happen to people," Kagan said.

The bells rang louder.

"Merry Christmas, Andrei."

"Whatever that means." Andrei thought about it. "The same to you, Pyotyr. Merry Christmas."

Acknowledgments

Special thanks are due to the residents of the Canyon Road area of Santa Fe, which includes Acequia Madre, Garcia, Camino del Monte Sol, and other adjoining streets. Each Christmas Eve, they transform their neighborhood into a fabulous seasonal delight that attracts visitors from around the world. Their hard work, good cheer, and holiday hospitality are much appreciated. The American Planning Association deservedly lists Canyon Road as one of the top-ten streets in the United States.

In addition, I'm indebted to the following people:

Mary Kay Andrews, whose charming holiday novel, *Blue Christmas,* prompted a conversation in which she suggested I write a Christmas book about a spy;

C. J. Lyons, an exciting novelist *(Lifelines)* and specialist in pediatric emergency medicine, who told me about emergency substitutes for baby formula as well as other details about infant care that were handy for my main character to know;

Roger Cooper, Peter Costanzo, Georgina Levitt, Amanda Ferber, and the wonderfully supportive group at Vanguard Press/Perseus Books;

My editor, Steve Saffel;

My publicist, Sarie Morrell, and my Internet guide, Nanci Kalanta; and

Jane Dystel, Miriam Goderich, and the rest of the good folks at Dystel/Goderich Literary Management.

All of these people light my path.

—*David Morrell*

ABOUT THE AUTHOR

David Morrell is the award-winning author of *First Blood*, the novel in which the character Rambo was created. He was born in 1943 in Kitchener, Ontario, Canada. In 1960, at the age of seventeen, he became a fan of the classic television series *Route 66*, about two young men in a Corvette convertible traveling the United States in search of America and themselves. The scripts by Stirling Silliphant so impressed Morrell that he decided to become a writer.

In 1966, the work of another writer, Hemingway scholar Philip Young, prompted Morrell to move to the United States, where he studied with Young at the Pennsylvania State University and received his M.A. and Ph.D. in American literature. There he also met the Golden Age science-fiction writer William Tenn (real name Philip Klass), who taught Morrell

the basics of fiction writing. The result was *First Blood*, a
novel about a returned Vietnam veteran suffering from post-
traumatic stress disorder who comes into conflict with a
small-town police chief and fights his own version of the
Vietnam War.

That "father" of modern action novels was published in
1972 while Morrell was a professor in the English department at the University of Iowa. He taught there from 1970 to
1986, simultaneously writing other novels, many of them
New York Times bestsellers, including the classic spy trilogy
The Brotherhood of the Rose (the basis for a top-rated NBC
miniseries broadcast after the Super Bowl), *The Fraternity of
the Stone*, and *The League of Night and Fog*.

Eventually wearying of two professions, Morrell gave up
his tenure in order to write full time. Shortly afterward, his
fifteen-year-old son Matthew was diagnosed with a rare form
of bone cancer and died in 1987, a loss that haunts not only
Morrell's life but his work, as in his memoir about Matthew,
Fireflies, and his novel *Desperate Measures*, whose main character has lost a son.

"The mild-mannered professor with the bloody-minded visions," as one reviewer called him, Morrell is the author of
thirty books, including such high-action thrillers as *The Fifth
Profession*, *Assumed Identity*, and *Extreme Denial* (set in Santa
Fe, New Mexico, where he now lives with his wife, Donna).
His *The Successful Novelist: A Lifetime of Lessons about Writing
and Publishing* analyzes what he has learned during his almost four decades as an author.

Morrell is the cofounder of the International Thriller Writers organization. Noted for his research, he is a graduate of the National Outdoor Leadership School for wilderness survival as well as the G. Gordon Liddy Academy of Corporate Security. In addition, he is an honorary lifetime member of the Special Operations Association and the Association for Intelligence Officers. He has been trained in firearms, hostage negotiation, assuming identities, executive protection, and offensive/defensive driving, among numerous other action skills that he describes in his novels. With eighteen million copies in print, his work has been translated into twenty-six languages.

Morrell is a three-time recipient of the distinguished Bram Stoker Award, the latest for his novel *Creepers*. Comic-Con International honored him with its prestigious Inkpot Award for his lifetime contributions to popular culture. You can visit him at www.davidmorrell.net.